THE EX

DANIELLE GIRARD

ALSO BY DANIELLE GIRARD

DR. ANNABELLE SCHWARTZMAN SERIES
Exhume
Excise
Expose
Expire

BADLANDS THRILLER SERIES
White Out
Far Gone
Up Close (coming 2023)

THE ROOKIE CLUB SERIES

Dead Center
One Clean Shot
Dark Passage
Grave Danger
Everything to Lose

OTHER WORKS
Savage Art
Ruthless Game
Chasing Darkness
Cold Silence

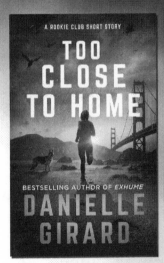

Advanced Praise for *The Ex*

"A writer whose work sucks me in and doesn't let me go, Danielle's newest story is a humdinger! Annabelle Schwartzman is a superb ME and Danielle is at the top of her game."

—JT Ellison,
New York Times bestselling author of *Her Dark Lies*

"*The Ex* is both a compelling character study and murder mystery, giving fans of Girard's Annabelle Schwartzman series a closer look at their beloved ME... a brilliant stand-alone work of psychological suspense that is sure to satisfy lovers of all crime genres."

—Wendy Walker,
bestselling author of *Don't Look For Me*

"Prepare to be wowed by *The Ex*! Page-turning action combined with fully-realized characters makes this Schwartzman saga a compulsively readable, heart-wrenching story I couldn't put down!"

— DJ Palmer,
USA Today bestselling author of *My Wife is Missing*

"*The Ex* is the first Danielle Girard book I've read, and I am now going to snap up her entire backlist. With the perfect blend of emotion and suspense, excellent pacing, and a compelling, wonderfully vivid protagonist, Girard has created a gripping story of strength and conviction. She grabs your attention from the first line, keeping you captive until the tense, brilliant ending."

—Samantha M. Bailey,
USA Today and #1 national bestselling
author of *Watch Out For Her*

"This story is a compelling and heart-breaking treasure. Only the talented Danielle Girard could combine a devious murder mystery with such an intense undercurrent of emotional depth. Empathy mixes with expertise in this riveting and original tale of marriage and motherhood and murder—and we are shown the hope that can come from survival. Do not miss this!"

—Hank Phillippi Ryan,
USA Today bestselling author of *Her Perfect Life*

"Fans of Girard's Annabelle Schwartzman series rejoice! Everyone's favorite ME is back in *The Ex*, an expertly plotted and fast-paced addition to the series, a read-in-one sitting thriller."

— Kimberly Belle,
internationally bestselling author of *My Darling Husband*

"A tense, emotional suspense loaded with character development and a smartly woven plot that will have you questioning everything you think you know."

—Jaime Lynn Hendricks,
bestselling author of *Finding Tessa* and *It Could Be Anyone*

"I fell in love with Dr. Annabelle Schwartzman from the very first page and devoured *The Ex* in one sitting. A gut-wrenching story of trauma and mystery told with impeccable detail and expertise. Schwartzman is officially my new favorite medical examiner and I can't wait to dive into the series."

— Lucinda Berry,
bestselling author of *Under Her Care* and *The Best of Friends*

"A pitch-perfect mystery that will grip both existing fans of the series and those who are new to Annabelle Schwartzman alike. I raced through *The Ex* in one thrilling sitting and you will too."

—Lisa Gray,
bestselling author of the *Jessica Shaw Series*

"*The Ex* by Danielle Girard packs so much emotion it'll stay with you long after you've finished reading. Shocking and disturbing, yet tender and caring, the descriptions and characters are so vivid and real, it's as if you're by Dr. Annabelle Schwartzman side. A haunting, terrific read."

—Hannah Mary McKinnon,
internationally bestselling author of *Never Coming Home*

"This story, full of deep grief, menacing memory, and pure suspense, will grab you and haunt you long after you've put it down. Girard is a master at weaving dangerous emotion with cold science, leaving her readers breathless. And if you haven't met Dr. Annabelle Schwartzman, prepare to be obsessed."

—Jennifer Pashley,
award winning author of *The Watcher*

"*The Ex* is a fast-paced, heart-wrenching read. San Francisco medical examiner Annabelle Schwartzman is back, better than ever. Her caseload includes a poisoned politician, the case she is supposed to focus on, and a pregnant young woman, Diane Reilly, a suspected suicide. Annabelle's drawn to Reilly's case for reasons made clear through poignant and terrifying flashbacks of her stalker ex Spencer. A quick, propulsive story. Fans of the series will love it."

—Kaira Rouda,
USA Today and Amazon Charts bestselling author
of T*he Next Wife* and *Somebody's Home*

"Clear your afternoon—once you begin this fast-paced, utterly engrossing novella, you won't be able to put it down! Danielle Girard skillfully weaves a puzzling mystery together with scenes of emotional heft, resulting in a compelling, highly satisfying read."

—Kathleen Barber,
author of *Truth Be Told*

For the readers who love Annabelle as much as I do,
this story is for you

Wearing a sterile Tyvek suit over her slacks and short-sleeved blouse, Annabelle Schwartzman set her ME case beside the bed. Through the bedroom window, the setting sun cast an orange glow on two neighboring apartment buildings. A thick beam of sunlight highlighted the bedroom wall, exposing years of fingerprints and a constellation of tiny nail holes where pictures and art had once hung.

The apartment where Diane Reilly lived with her boyfriend was in a swanky area of San Francisco called Cow Hollow. Although small, the apartment was comfortable and appointed in the way of young couples in the city, some combination of Pottery Barn and IKEA. From the dust along the baseboards behind the bureau and the bedside table, Annabelle suspected the couple had lived here for some time. That was common for people in San Francisco where rent was astronomical and staying in one place meant reaping the benefits of rent control. The bedroom was messy, typical of busy people, but nothing she saw suggested a struggle.

Annabelle shifted her attention to the victim. Though the position in San Francisco was her first official M.E. job, she'd worked as an examiner for almost four years in residency and she felt comfortable in the presence of the dead. While some medical examiners barely looked at a body prior to opening their kit and setting to work, Annabelle wasn't one of them. For her, first impressions were crucial. It was one of the reasons the job was harder when the body had been moved.

Diane Reilly, however, lay where she had died in her bed. A heavy blanket was pushed to one side, the comforter and sheets bunched at her feet when the paramedics had examined her and determined she was beyond their help. Although she was slumped to her left side in death, it appeared that she had been sitting upright with pillows propped behind her. The two remote controls on the bed beside the body suggested she had been watching television. With her eyes closed, Reilly might have been asleep except for the bluish tint of her lips. On the bedside table was an empty prescription bottle of oxycodone in the name of Peter Nelson and a tall opaque glass with a white straw. The bottom of the glass was coated with a watered-down, milky residue and with her hands gloved, Annabelle lifted the glass to her nose. Mint. She studied the small bits of dark in the residue. A mint chocolate chip milkshake, if she had to guess.

Annabelle swiped the thermometer across the victim's forehead. Her temperature was 95.9, suggesting she'd been dead less than two hours. The room was warm—the thermostat read 74—so the decline in temperature should have been about 1.5 degrees per hour. Annabelle's watch read 7:19, which indicated Reilly had likely died between 5:30 and 6 p.m. Identifying such a narrow window for time of death was rare and could make it easier to determine cause. A lucky break.

Annabelle propped a Tyvek-covered knee on the bed and reached across to examine the victim's head and neck for signs of contusion, but the skull was undamaged and the cervical vertebrae seemed perfectly aligned. Nothing to suggest injury. Annabelle pushed up the victim's sweatshirt sleeves one at a time to check the skin on the hands and forearms. There was no apparent bruising, no lacerations, no needle marks; only a single, thin Band-Aid wrapped around the middle finger of the left hand. Annabelle removed it and found a shallow cut. The epidermis was closed and whatever inflammation there might have been was gone, suggesting the wound was at least a couple of days old. Kitchen accident, probably. All very mundane.

Next, Annabelle lifted the sweatshirt from the victim's waist, exposing her belly. At the sight, she drew back momentarily, feeling a heaviness in her own belly as her gaze locked on the fundal bump. The victim was pregnant. *I hate the pregnant ones.* From the main room, the sobs from Reilly's boyfriend grew louder.

Statistically speaking, a pregnant woman was less likely to commit suicide than a non-pregnant one. Annabelle couldn't recall where she'd read that, and it might not matter here. Recognizing her own bias, she worked to put it in check, to push her own memories aside; pregnant victims were hard for everyone.

"Anything noteworthy?"

Annabelle jumped at the voice and stood from the bed. Across the room, Hal Harris's bulk filled the doorway. At 6'4" and somewhere north of 220 pounds, Harris was an imposing figure. His flawless dark skin made his hazel eyes green, especially in bright light, and his stern expression suggested that he was not someone to mess with. Behind the façade, however, Hal was both easygoing and extremely kind; although Annabelle tried to avoid favoritism, Hal was her favorite homicide inspector.

"I'm still doing the initial exam," Annabelle said. "Won't know until I have her at the morgue."

"Looks like an overdose, right?" Hal asked. "Boyfriend's real broken up." He rubbed his bald head the way he did when he was thinking. "Girlfriend kills herself… and she was pregnant."

Momentarily breathless, Annabelle stooped down to her ME case and removed the top shelf, setting it on the floor to retrieve her notebook. She moved slowly, conscious of her own flat belly, giving herself time to gain control of the memories that threatened to drown her.

Hal lifted the glass from the bedside table. "What's this?"

"Mint chocolate chip milkshake, I think," Annabelle said, her heart rate slowly returning to normal. "Or it was, anyway."

Hal sniffed the glass before setting it on the table. "A milkshake, huh? One last treat on her way out?"

Something about the notion of making a milkshake in order to commit suicide struck Annabelle as odd, and she felt her bias stretch out a suspicious tentacle. "Prescription's in the name of Peter Nelson."

"Nelson's the boyfriend," Hal confirmed.

She rose slowly and opened her notebook, her pen poised as she nodded toward the doorway and the man who could still be heard crying from the other room. "He tell you what happened?"

"They were supposed to go to the neighborhood's annual block party today," Hal said. "At the last minute, she says she's not up for it, so he goes alone. He's only gone about an hour and when he comes in, he finds her."

Hal handed over the victim's driver's license. Annabelle scanned it for the woman's date of birth, still getting used to the appearance of the California licenses. June 24th. The victim would have been twenty-nine in a few weeks.

"Boyfriend says there's a history of depression in her family," Hal said, cutting into her thoughts. "She was on an antidepressant for years. Got off when she found out she was pregnant."

Annabelle made a note to check the victim's medical records.

"I've got patrol talking to some of the neighbors to confirm his alibi, but seems pretty cut and dried," Hal continued. "History of depression, off her meds..." He looked around the room. "Unless you find something else, we can close this one pretty fast.

Which is good news, because I need you to go over the Fischer autopsy again."

Fischer was a local politician, poisoned three nights ago while eating dinner at his favorite restaurant. There'd been sixty other diners, along with a staff of twenty-four, in the building at the time.

"We need to see if we missed anything," Hal continued, stifling a yawn. "You think you'll have time for that tomorrow?"

"I'll try to get to it," she told him. She nodded toward the living room where the boyfriend was still crying. "He mention how far along she was?" she asked, lowering her voice.

"Sixteen weeks."

Annabelle wrote "16 weeks" in her notebook, then "28 years old." She studied the victim's face. No bags beneath her eyes, no gaunt cheeks—none of the physical signs that should go along with suicide. This victim seemed at peace, as if she were resting, but Annabelle knew there was no single look for a suicide. Perhaps this woman had decided life was too much, or maybe there was something amiss. Annabelle tried to stop her mind from running in circles. Making something out of nothing because of her own past was the last thing she could afford to do.

Annabelle returned to the victim and lifted her hands, studying them a second time. Still she found no defensive wounds. Was there something she was missing?

"You see anything?" Hal asked.

Annabelle glanced up. "Not yet." Why was she resisting the idea that Diane Reilly had killed herself? Pregnant women committed suicide. "Anything else I should know?"

"They've been together since college," Hal continued. "He's been out of work since last October, so she was supporting them. Think that's about all."

"I'll draw blood so we can run a tox screen. Can't hurt to check for other drugs or alcohol," she said.

"Maybe she just didn't want a baby."

Annabelle paused, then turned to Hal. "At sixteen weeks, you've got other options." At least in *this* state women did.

"True." Hal rubbed his scalp again. "Maybe she didn't see a way out? Depression does that."

"Yes," she agreed. Depression would certainly explain the suicide. She set the victim's hands onto the bed, then lifted one of the remote controls, aimed it at the TV, and hit the power button. The Netflix logo appeared in the center of the black screen. With the other remote control, Annabelle hit play.

"What are you doing?" Hal asked.

"Remote control was in bed with her. Looks like she was watching something when she died. I was curious about what it was." Annabelle nodded to the Netflix home screen. "Did the boyfriend mention shutting off the television after he found her?"

"He didn't," Hal said, making a note in his book. "I'll follow up." Hal cocked one eyebrow at her as his mouth bent into a frown. "You're thinking it wasn't suicide."

"I don't know," she admitted.

Hal exhaled. "Man, I need this one to be easy." The screen filled with the image of a blond woman frozen midstride, one hand raised. "*27 Dresses*," Hal read. "Can't say I know it."

"Cheesy chick flick," she told him.

"It help answer your question?"

She tried to recall the movie's plot. Something about always a bridesmaid, never a bride. "Not really."

Hal scanned the room. "You need anything else from here?"

"Just blood samples."

Hal nodded and Annabelle focused on the body. They didn't talk as Annabelle collected blood and scraped the inside of the victim's cheek. As she was packing up her case, the crime scene unit entered, making the room suddenly crowded. Hal made his way out to talk to the team leader. As Annabelle walked toward the front door, she caught sight of the boyfriend, seated on the couch. Head in his hands, he glanced over and caught her eye. Annabelle studied his expression but found it unreadable.

As an afterthought, she returned to the couple's bedroom and crossed to the only closet in the room. She scanned the row of clothes—all women's. His were likely in the front hall closet. In tiny San Francisco apartments, closet space was at a premium and, in Annabelle's experience, women seemed to stake claim to the largest spaces.

A laundry basket on the floor contained a few items, including a pair of boxer shorts on top, which suggested they shared the hamper. Shoes were lined neatly on a metal rack; belts hung on one wall, purses on two oversized hooks, and the shelves were occupied by large clear storage bins. Maybe clothes for other seasons. Nothing unusual.

Annabelle found Hal in the hallway and opened the closet there. As she suspected, it was full of men's clothes. When she turned to Hal, he motioned toward the kitchen. "There's a blender on the counter. I'll make sure it gets collected, too."

"I'll do the autopsy in the morning and give you a call before noon."

"Thanks," Hal said.

As she started to walk away, he added, "And you'll take another look at Fischer?"

"As soon as I can," she said.

"Tomorrow would be amazing."

Annabelle said nothing. Whatever she did tomorrow, Diane Reilly got priority over the politician.

★

Annabelle was in the morgue before seven. She had slept fitfully, interrupted by disjointed dreams, and at half past five, she gave up on sleep and got out of bed. It would be a busy day with two autopsies to perform and a stack of cases to review, including Fischer's. Reilly first, though. The sooner she finished the autopsy, the sooner she could move past her own memories, which rose like floodwater when a case hit this close to home.

She wanted to say it was a straightforward case. Hal was an experienced inspector and he seemed to buy the boyfriend's story, but whatever either of them believed made no difference to her process. One of the first rules of her job was "Never expect a specific outcome."

The morgue was cooler than usual, so she adjusted the heat and kept her sweater on under her lab coat in the hope that either she or the room would soon warm up. The extra layer of clothing made her movements awkward.

She slid Diane Reilly's body from the cold storage drawer and noted that the body bag and Reilly's clothes had been removed, taken to the lab for processing. That meant there should also be a full set of X-rays, so Annabelle booted her computer. The machine kicked and hissed as it launched. Though it was new, the morgue computer always acted like it was an ancient beast, frustrated to be put to work. Annabelle waited until her login appeared, typed in the complicated password, and launched the program to view Reilly's file.

While the files loaded, Annabelle stared at the shape of the body under the sheet, then drew the cloth down over her face to confirm identity. Through the sheet, the bulge of the victim's pregnancy was obvious and Annabelle flashed back to lying in that cold hospital room. The doctor who had come into the room that day was one she'd never seen before. And never saw again.

"Your cervix is dilated, Mrs. MacDonald," the doctor had announced, just past three a.m. "It's time now."

Annabelle had clenched her fists and shaken her head, tightening her abdomen against the overwhelming desire to push—as though if she could hold it in, everything might be all right.

Standing in the morgue, Annabelle smoothed the sheet over the edge of the autopsy table, tempted to simply leave the bottom half of the body covered until it was necessary to remove it for examination. But she never left a body covered, not even the worst floaters or ones with the most gruesome wounds. Her rule was to display the entire body and view it as a whole.

Reilly should be no different.

"It's just another victim," Annabelle whispered to herself as she folded the sheet down across the victim's belly, then over again to her shins. From there, it was easy to fold into a small square.

Annabelle held the folded sheet against her abdomen and forced herself to look at Diane Reilly. To really study her body. Her breasts were swollen, light blue veins visible beneath the skin. Annabelle could almost feel the weight in her own breasts—the tenderness, the extra sensitivity that had made them feel like they were individual, living things when she was pregnant.

The nurse had seemed so young, even to her twenty-eight-year-old self. Standing above the hospital bed, the nurse had patted Annabelle's forehead with a wet cloth until Annabelle pushed her away. "I want my husband," she had said, closing her eyes to the pain, which was an excruciating wave of pressure, like being pinned under a car. Everything ceased with the weight of it. Her lungs drew no air; her heart didn't beat. For one. Two. Three. And then slowly, the weight eased off. Her heart restarted with a tremendous thump. Her lungs sucked hungrily at the air, her jaw unclenching momentarily. "Please," she begged. "Spencer should be here."

"Don't fight it, Mrs. MacDonald," the doctor said. "You're almost there."

"I have to wait for him," she said breathlessly.

An older nurse came to the bed. "He can't be here, honey." Her hip pressed against Annabelle as she stretched her arms up to change out the IV.

Annabelle strained to see the monitor. In the past week, she had started to feel the baby. The sensation, like tiny champagne bubbles rising inside her belly or the fluttering wings of tiny butterflies, had made her feel warm and loved. Now there was only a devastating stillness. "Is there any change?" she asked. "Do you see her moving? Her heartbeat?"

"No, honey," the nurse said. "I'm afraid not."

Annabelle fell back onto the pillow and covered her eyes, letting the tears fall. "Why do I have to push, then? What difference does it make if she's…?" But she couldn't say the word.

The doctor stood at the foot of the bed, adjusting bright blue gloves over short, stubby fingers. "It'll be done soon, Annabelle. You can do this."

The doctor looked small and insignificant beside the nurse, who was tying his gown behind him. He wasn't her regular doctor. Where was Dr. Foley?

He slapped his gloved hands together awkwardly like he was gearing up to make a play on a football field. Then he was between her legs and she felt his hand. "We're ready to push," the doctor announced.

The morgue computer let out a short double beep as Reilly's file loaded on the screen. Annabelle scanned the contents, but aside from a full set of X-rays that would have been taken earlier this morning, the file was mostly empty. Hal had yet to upload the victim's medical history or the doctor's contact information. Annabelle eyed the file folder of Reilly's X-ray images and considered taking a peek, but decided she would do her own exam first. She was a creature of habit, someone who appreciated a specific order to her process. First the body, then the background material, just as she would work any other case.

Standing beside the body, Annabelle touched the globe of the victim's pregnancy with her gloved palm. "Okay, we're going to start now," she said, then allowed a moment to pass, her way of honoring the dead. Without allowing herself time for any more second-guessing, Annabelle started the video recording. As she always did, she began at the head, using a penlight to check the ears then the nose, but her focus kept shifting to the pregnant bump. With the penlight switched off, she slid it into her pocket and gave in to the distraction. *Get it over with.* She measured a line from the upper edge of the pubis bone to the peak of the womb.

"Fundal height is 13.5 inches," she said for the recording, lifting the tape to show the camera the distance she had measured. She used the calculator to divide the height by .8, which gave an estimate of the pregnancy in weeks: 16.75, in this case. By that measurement, Diane Reilly's pregnancy had lasted five days longer than Annabelle's own. The fetal measurements would be a better indicator, but the number was consistent with what the boyfriend had told Hal.

Returning to the victim's head, Annabelle again drew the penlight from her breast pocket and continued the autopsy as she would any victim, by checking the orifices. "Eyes and nose clear," she reported. Rigor mortis had set into the jaw muscles, but with some wiggling, Annabelle was able to break the rigor and open the jaw. She collected some residue from the teeth, which she suspected was chocolate, and scraped it onto a clean white sheet of butcher paper, noting where it had come from and the time.

There was also a white chalky substance around the teeth and gums which Annabelle collected with dental floss. The appearance was consistent with oxycodone pills. The fact that it was in her teeth suggested she had chewed the pills rather than swallowing them whole. Annabelle considered that for a moment, imagining the bitter taste—though the milkshake would have helped with that. But why chew them? Had Diane Reilly worried that she might vomit before they were absorbed if she swallowed them whole? That her suicide attempt might fail? She made a note to mention it to Hal.

Bagging and labeling the evidence from the mouth, Annabelle moved on to the victim's largest organ, the skin. With a small, magnified light source, she went over the body in search of any contusions. She began at the upper arms, which commonly showed signs of grip marks in an abusive relationship. But Reilly showed no bruising there. None on the thighs or near the hands or wrists, which might have suggested an attempt at restraint. In fact, there were no contusions anywhere other than a single bruise on the victim's left tibia. Measurement from the bottom of the foot to the contusion was sixteen inches, consistent with the height of a coffee table.

Annabelle made note of the injury for the video, then moved the victim onto her left side to examine her posterior. Again nothing. No marks on her back or buttocks, nothing to suggest that she had been mistreated.

The external exam completed, Annabelle eased the victim onto her back, shut off the recording, and discarded her gloves. She pulled her chair up to the computer and shifted her attention to the file with the X-ray images. She studied them in the same order she had examined the body, beginning with the head. The skull was fine; the brain appeared undamaged and there were no injuries to the vertebrae. Same with the torso and right arm. At the discovery of a hairline fracture across the left radius, Annabelle zoomed in the image for a closer look. Of the body's 206 bones, the radius was one of the most commonly broken. In Reilly's case, a callus had formed at the site of the fracture, so the break was not recent. Annabelle zoomed in further and noted small calcium deposits in the callus; the presence of calcium aged the break further. The injury was a decade old, maybe more. There was nothing at all notable in the rest of the X-rays. The only injury Reilly appeared to have sustained in her almost twenty-nine years was a single fracture to her wrist.

Starting to consider she might have been wrong on this one, Annabelle continued her exam by retrieving the camera from the storage closet and connecting the long-wave UV light filter to the lens. Its rays penetrated deeper into the skin, enabling her to see older injuries, as far back as five months. There was nothing about Reilly's presentation that suggested the need for further investigation, so she did this exercise without recording it. The department lauded their staff for being thorough, but taking this additional step without cause might appear like a waste of time. If she found something, she would retake the images with the recording device on, but right now, she was simply curious.

No, she was *suspicious*, but she was beginning to believe her suspicion was unreasonable. After each shot, Annabelle zoomed in and inspected the image on the camera's LED screen. More than fifty images and nothing came up to suggest Diane Reilly had been abused. Annabelle put the camera away and tried to isolate what it was about this case that was so bothersome.

There was nothing in the external exam to indicate foul play, so why didn't she want to believe Reilly's death was a suicide?

Suddenly, Annabelle wanted this autopsy done so she could put it aside and move on.

Shifting her focus to the work, she rolled her equipment tray to the cabinet and selected sterilized scalpels in three sizes, two sets of forceps—one pair of dissecting forceps and one of toothed—and two pairs of scissors. The pruning shears she would use to cut through the ribs were already by the autopsy table. She scanned the bins for anything else she might need and saw two pairs of infant skull shears in a bin of their own. She would not autopsy the fetus. Hopefully there would be no need.

Setting aside everything else, Annabelle went to work, and in a little over two hours, she had completed the initial autopsy on Diane Reilly, except for the last remaining piece—the fetus. The clock on the wall said nine-twenty. Annabelle was hungry, and she knew she wouldn't be once she began the autopsy of the uterus. She pulled off her gloves and shut off the recording equipment, telling herself to take a break. *Get some food, some coffee. Come back to this.*

But she found she couldn't walk away. Instead, she reached for fresh gloves and switched on the recorder again. *Get it over with.*

Scalpel in hand, she allowed herself several shaky breaths before laying her hand on the rounded bump of Diane Reilly's abdomen and making an initial incision.

Although the fetus was still very small, Annabelle made her incisions with the utmost care to avoid damaging the tiny form then set her tools down on the table to free her hands. As she removed the body, roughly the size of a nectarine, the first thing she noticed was the small mound between the skinny, translucent legs. A boy.

Annabelle cut the umbilical cord and retrieved a clean cloth, using one hand to spread it out on the metal table beside the victim. She cupped the fetus in two hands for several seconds, feeling the tiny weight of the budding life before setting him on the scale. "Fetal weight, 119.3 grams," she said for the recording, then laid the infant on the cloth on the metal table beside his mother. She pulled the sheet over the two bodies and returned mother and son to cold storage.

By the time she walked through the morgue's heavy door, Annabelle was desperate for fresh air. She drew a deep breath as she walked down the hall. The pungent scent of lilies made her suddenly nauseous, and her mind buzzed with a swarm of images: flower arrangements perched on the country club's marble tabletops and sidebars, a sea of dark wood polished to perfect reflection.

On her way out of the building, Annabelle passed the front desk where an oversized bouquet of white lilies sat perched on the counter. Smell was the strongest trigger of memory, she knew, and so she tried not to inhale, even though the scent had already flooded her olfactory glands and overwhelmed her with the memories of that day. She moved past swiftly, offering a quick wave when the receptionist said good morning.

On the street, the smell of coffee and fresh pastries mixed with the lilies, and another unbeckoned memory returned from seven years ago.

The country club had smelled of fresh cinnamon cake. She was twenty-eight, and five years married. Though she had her degree from Duke by then, she didn't work outside the home. That was how Spencer explained her role. "Annabelle doesn't work outside the home," he would say, as if managing his home, with the help of his live-in housekeeper Trudy, was a career in its own right.

Her husband had linked his arm in hers and squeezed her hand gently as they made their way along the club's long hallway. He knew those situations made her uncomfortable, but she suspected his attention was more related to what had happened the night before and how others might judge them if they knew. It was essential to Spencer that he always appear the doting husband.

"Look, Tamara's already here," he whispered, patting her hand as if she were a kindergartner on her first day of school. Making her feel like one.

Tamara's husband, Gregory, was one of Spencer's partners and Spencer had made it clear that he considered Tamara a good role model. The ideal Southern mother. Her four children stood in a straight line whenever the family was all together, the youngest held in the arms of the oldest, their matching Lily Pulitzer outfits starched and pressed.

As though she'd heard her name, Tamara Whitman glanced up from the table where she sat and waved. She stood as they approached, clapping her hands silently. "I'm so glad you're here, Annabelle. This will be so much fun."

Spencer wanted a family like Whitman's. To that end, he had set his wife up as a sort of intern to Tamara Whitman's life.

"May I?" Tamara asked, already moving in with both palms to cup Annabelle's growing belly. "Do you feel her moving?"

"More and more," Annabelle said, relaxing a bit.

"You're going to be so thrilled to have a girl first. They're so helpful when the younger ones come along."

"Okay, Tamara," Spencer said. "I'm leaving my gorgeous bride in your capable hands."

Annabelle flinched as Spencer's elbow grazed the fresh wound on her arm.

His eyes flashed wide before narrowing in anger.

She cupped her hand over her arm and shook her head to assure him it was nothing. She was pretty sure the scab had not broken open.

"I'll take good care of her, I promise," Tamara told him with a wink, seeming oblivious to his flash of anger.

"I should be home around seven," Spencer told Annabelle, kissing her cheek.

"Maybe we should all meet for dinner," Tamara suggested. "I'd have to check Gregory's schedule, but I think he's free tonight."

Spencer looked expectantly at Annabelle, and she felt a lurch in her chest as she shook her head. "Tonight is the Bill Bryson reading, remember?"

Through her thin linen jacket, his fingers found the butterfly sutures. She had wanted to use superglue to close the wound, but Spencer had worried it might be bad for the baby. "You wouldn't want to hurt our daughter," he'd said, helping her apply sutures to the wound he had *just caused. When it was done, he had taken her hands, real tears in his eyes. "I can't live without you, Bella."*

"You don't have to," she'd told him.

"I know," he had responded—and, as if the tears had been a mirage, his eyes were dry. His gaze had grown fierce then, heated. "It makes me so happy to know we'll always be together."

She had merely nodded; he'd seemed so close to another explosion of violence. Now, she stood with Tamara and Spencer, afraid to speak.

"Bill Bryson?" Tamara asked, breaking the silence. Her broad smile was unfailing.

"He's written a few books," she said. "A Small History of Nearly Everything," *she added softly. "He's speaking tonight." A moment passed and Annabelle felt compelled to keep talking. "He's quite good, actually. My aunt turned me onto him. That book lays out the history of the planet in a very accessible way. There's so much of it that I didn't understand until—"*

Spencer slowly squeezed the wound on her arm.

Annabelle stopped talking and noticed the expression on Tamara's face. Surprise, or perhaps confusion.

Spencer's hold tightened until the sharp sting of the fresh wound splitting open brought tears to her eyes. "Bella considers herself quite the academic," Spencer said, his disdain barely hidden by a smile that didn't reach his eyes.

Tamara laughed politely. Annabelle tried to join in, but the sound fell into something more like a cough.

"Dinner another time," Spencer said, finally loosening his grip. "Goodbye, ladies."

Annabelle stood in silence as her husband disappeared down the hall. Then, her arm throbbing, she sat down at the table. She tucked her purse under her chair, smoothed the edge of the white linen table-cloth, and scanned the rows of name tags lined up along its surface.

Her heart was beating too fast to speak, and she was afraid to look at her arm for fear she was bleeding again.

"Are you feeling all right?" Tamara's eyes shifted from Annabelle's belly back to her face.

"Absolutely," Annabelle lied.

"I never felt better in my entire life than when I was pregnant," said Tamara, a dreamy note in her voice.

For Annabelle, pregnancy hadn't come with the magic glow other women raved about. She cast about for a suitable reply and was glad for the distraction when an elderly woman approached the table, using a cane for support.

"Hello, Mrs. Cardwell, and welcome to the annual Children's Library Tea," Tamara said, then turned to Annabelle and made the introductions.

Carefully, Annabelle fingered the cut on her arm. He'd been cutting a lime for his drink. She couldn't remember what she'd said, but there had been the slightest shift in Spencer's expression an instant before he jabbed the knife into her arm.

As blood ran in a slow stream to her elbow and dripped onto the floor, Annabelle's first thought had been how much the lime juice made it sting.

Annabelle made a tick mark on the list next to Mrs. Cardwell's name as Tamara handed her a printed name badge. "We want to thank you for your support this year."

"I'm always happy to support the children's fund," the woman said as she peeled the sticker backing from her badge and reached to press it to her blouse.

Tamara leapt up from the table. "Oh, no, Mrs. Cardwell! You'll ruin that silk if you stick that there."

The older woman jerked her hand away and stared at the sticker attached to her thumb as though it were dangerous.

Tamara took the sticker from Mrs. Cardwell and pressed it neatly onto a clear plastic badge holder with a small metal clip, then fastened the badge to the older woman's collar.

The woman patted it and smiled. "Thank you very much, dear."

"My pleasure." Tamara gripped the woman's hand as though they were co-conspirators. "I always keep a few of the plastic ones for anyone who's wearing silk."

"Very clever of you." Mrs. Cardwell lifted her cane and made her way toward the ballroom.

When Tamara sat back down, she was pale. Tiny beads of sweat lined her upper lip and her mouth sat in a flat line.

"I'm so sorry," Annabelle said. "I didn't even think about it."

Tamara raised her wine glass and took a long sip before setting it down. "I did that to a blouse once."

Annabelle waited.

Tamara pressed her eyes closed. "It was awful."

Annabelle sensed something dark in her voice.

Tamara took another drink. "It was a gift to me from an important client of Gregory's."

Annabelle watched the woman beside her, waiting to make sense of this reaction. Had the client been angry—or Gregory? She sensed an opening and felt desperate to confide in someone. Would this woman understand what Spencer was?

She had opened her mouth to ask when two women appeared in the hall.

Using four fingertips, Tamara dabbed lightly beneath her eyes, brushed the back of her hand across her lip, and took an audible breath, then sat up straight in her chair. A moment later, her full smile made it appear as though nothing had happened.

That had been the last time Annabelle saw Tamara, and the last day of her pregnancy.

Annabelle flinched at the feeling of a hand on her arm and turned to see Hal Harris standing beside her.

The frown deepened between his brows. "You okay?"

She nodded quickly, glancing around at her surroundings. She was inside the coffee shop, though she had no recollection of entering.

"What can we get you, ma'am?" Holding up a coffee cup and giving it a little shake, the barista wore a tight, impatient smile. "Something to drink?"

Her face was suddenly hot. "Just a tall drip coffee. Black, please." She fumbled for her wallet, paid, and shoved a dollar into the tip jar. As she started to walk away, the barista called after her, "Here's your black drip, ma'am."

Annabelle returned for the cup and offered the barista an apologetic smile as she headed for the door. As she crossed the shop, she was tempted to walk out and drop her coffee in the nearest trashcan, but instead, she waited for Hal to retrieve his drink from the end of the coffee bar.

"I'd love to sit for a few," Hal said, "but I've got to get back. You want to walk?"

She followed him out the door. With her free hand, she held her sweater tight around her neck as she raised the cup to her lips. Took a tiny sip to test the temperature. Hot. Very hot.

"Have you gotten a medical history on Reilly?" she asked as they made their way toward the department.

"Doctor wasn't available when I called," Hal said, pulling his phone from his pocket. He entered his passcode, thumbed across the screen, then shook his head. "I talked to a nurse who was supposed to email her chart, but doesn't look like I've gotten it yet. I did ask about the television and the boyfriend says he's pretty sure he shut it off when he was waiting for the paramedics. But he admitted it was all sort of a blur." Hal returned his phone to his pocket. "Have you started the autopsy?"

Annabelle nodded. "Found some white chalky residue in her

teeth. It's consistent with the oxycodone, but I haven't sent it down to the lab yet. Has Roger had a chance to run any tests on the glass she was drinking from?" Roger Sampers, the head of the lab, was a magician with evidence. If there was anything to find, Roger would find it.

"I don't think so," Hal said. "The lab's swamped and we've got all the evidence from Fischer on a rush. I'm pretty sure they're still working through the chef knives. Twelve different chefs in the kitchen that night, and each one had at least four knives." Hal blew out a breath. "Case is a nightmare."

"Have you talked to her parents? Reilly's, I mean."

"They're distraught, of course," he said. "Thought she was really excited about the baby. What does it mean if there's oxycodone in her teeth? There wasn't residue in the glass, was there?"

"I didn't see any, no, but it may have been rinsed out. That's why I want Roger to check."

"And residue in the glass would indicate she crushed the pills up and mixed them with the milkshake?" Hal asked. Annabelle opened her mouth, but he added, "Or someone else did."

She nodded. "Right."

"Okay," he went on. "And if we *don't* find the drug in the glass, it means—?"

"She might have chewed the pills," Annabelle answered.

Hal glanced at her, stepping aside to let a group pass them. "Why would she do that?"

"Possibly to make the drug act more quickly, to make it harder for someone to save her in case she was discovered."

"So *no* residue in the glass would eliminate the question of homicide," Hal said, following her logic. "Because it would mean she chewed the pills. Hard to make someone do that without leaving signs of force."

"Yes," she agreed. "There were no signs of injury or defensive wounds, so no indication that she was tied down and forced to chew them or anything."

"And nothing else to indicate foul play?"

"No," she admitted.

"I'll get Roger to test the glass so we can close this one." They reached the building and Hal pulled the door open for her.

"I'd also like to see her medical history before I make a final determination."

Hal paused in the doorway. "I've got fifteen more kitchen staff to interview, but I'll send it on as soon as I see it. And Fischer?" he added.

"You sure are pushing the Fischer case hard."

Hal blew out a breath. "Mayor wants to release a statement ASAP. Captain's on my ass and I don't have shit. I swear, I'm ready to punch through a wall."

"I'll take a look before the end of the day."

Hal smiled for the first time. "Thank you."

With that, he crossed the foyer and disappeared into the stairwell.

Back in the morgue, Annabelle avoided the bodies of Reilly and her son. Instead, she went to work on the more straightforward autopsy of a man hit by a drunk driver going 47 miles per hour in a 25 zone. In autopsy, Annabelle identified the presence of blood in the abdominal cavity, confirming her initial suspicion that the cause of death was a splenic rupture. The ruptured spleen had caused massive bleeding, and the blood had pooled in his abdominal cavity. As a result, the victim went into shock and died. Had the driver called 911, the bleeding might have been stopped and the victim likely wouldn't have died, a point the prosecutors would surely use in their case against the driver.

Over lunch, Annabelle sat in her office and reviewed her notes on Fischer, searching for anything new to add to the investigation.

Fischer had died from ingesting a poisonous mushroom known as the western North American destroying angel, scientific name *Amanita ocreata*. According to his chief of staff and his wife, Fischer had eaten at his favorite restaurant on Tuesday night. Wednesday and Thursday, he'd shown symptoms of food poisoning with diarrhea and vomiting. He'd remained at home and in bed both days. When his wife had contacted the chef to let him know, she was reassured that no one else had reported any illness.

After the symptoms of foodborne illness subsided, Fischer had experienced jaundice and delirium, with intermittent seizures by the end of the weekend. The timeline fit perfectly with mushroom toxicity. Fischer had died Monday, six days after eating at the restaurant. The one bit of luck in the whole case was that Fischer had taken a doggie bag of leftovers home, and they were still in his refrigerator when he died.

To an untrained eye, *Amanita ocreata* looked like a regular mushroom. Though its edges were flatter than the standard white mushroom, when chopped into small pieces it would be nearly impossible to notice the difference. Whoever fed Fischer the mushrooms had known what they were doing. Annabelle did a second pass of the lab results and the images from the autopsy, but nothing offered her any new insight.

She was still trying to come up with something for Hal when Reilly's medical history dropped into her inbox. Needing a break from Fischer, Annabelle turned her attention to the file. Reilly had been prescribed Celexa, an SSRI, for her depression. Cross-referencing the prescription database, Annabelle confirmed that Celexa was one of the selective serotonin reuptake inhibitors that were considered safe for pregnancy. Moving on, she read through the doctor's notes. *Informed patient of option to continue SSRI in G1. Patient confer w/ therapist q. wk.* The "G1" meant "gravida 1," indicating that this was Reilly's first pregnancy. The doctor and

Reilly had agreed that she would stop taking the medication but that Reilly would talk to her therapist weekly, presumably to keep a close watch on her depression during pregnancy.

So what had happened?

Annabelle scanned the report for the name of the therapist— Samantha Allen-Harker. She googled the phone number and dialed. When Allen-Harker didn't answer, Annabelle left a message requesting that the therapist return her call, then faxed over a subpoena to make the request official.

Focused on the Fischer file, Annabelle stared at images of a sample of the politician's liver as seen under a microscope for several minutes before her mind shifted to Reilly. The thought that entered her head was that she wanted to hold the baby again. *A fetus,* she told herself. But still, she wanted to hold him. It was unprofessional and still, she longed to feel the tiny weight in her arms. Her time was limited. If nothing came of her call with Reilly's therapist, Annabelle would be forced to call the death a suicide and release the bodies.

She locked her office door and walked back down the hall toward the morgue. The smell of the lilies had dissipated. For a fleeting moment, she wondered if she had imagined the bouquet, but she'd seen it, hadn't she?

Alone in the morgue, Annabelle pulled on her white lab coat and retrieved a fresh pair of gloves. She glanced toward the door. If someone came in and found her holding a victim's dead fetus, it would certainly raise questions, but medical examiners were known to work on hunches. She could simply say she was checking a theory, make something up if they pressed. She took hold of the drawer handle and pulled Reilly from the wall, then folded down the side of the sheet to reveal the unborn infant. She felt something hard lodge in her throat as she lifted him off the small cloth, cupping his naked form in her hands.

She turned on the magnifying lamp and studied his thin, waxy skin; saw the hint of hair follicles along his arms and on the tiny rounded mound of his shoulders. On his head, wisps of hair were beginning to grow. She studied the color of his irises, which were visible through the translucent skin of his eyelids. But mostly, she just appreciated the weight of him in her hand, lighter than her cell phone.

"I want to hold her," Annabelle had said, lying in the sterile hospital bed. Chilled under the thin blanket, she was desperate to sleep. The weight pulling her eyes closed was enormous, but she fought it by wiggling her fingers and toes. Fingers, then toes, then fingers again. She would not close her eyes until she held her baby. "May I see her, please?" she repeated.

"Of course, Mrs. MacDonald," came the nurse's gravelly voice. "We're getting things cleaned up a bit."

"Things." Her baby was not a "she." She was a "thing." No, that wasn't right. Even dead, Olivia was her baby girl. The nurse appeared at her bedside, a furrow cut deep between her dark eyebrows as she handed over the tiny bundle.

Annabelle had trembled as she took the blanket. Only the slightest weight indicated there was anything wrapped inside. Without looking, she closed her eyes and held the bundle to her chest. Her breasts were heavy, the front of her gown damp where the colostrum offered itself to her baby. She had been surprised that it had come so soon, when she was months from her due date. But her body knew—knew she was a mother. She had a daughter and already she was being forced to bury her.

Grief struck a punch to her chest, making it hard to breathe. Annabelle pressed her nose to the blanket, hoping for a scent of her child, but what she smelled was the faint scent of fabric softener. Her arms rocked slowly as though of their own volition. Her plan had been to learn all the lullabies prior to Olivia's birth. She never had the chance. The only one she knew was "Rock-a-Bye Baby." She hummed it softly into the blanket. "And down will come baby, cradle and all."

Shifting the bundle into the crook of her left arm, she slowly unwrapped the blanket. A sob caught in her throat as she folded down the last bit of fleece and broke free in a violent wave of tears. Her baby was so small, barely the size of a pear. Her head seemed to make up more than a third of her, tiny blue veins visible through her scalp, her skin almost transparent. Her arms and legs were barely thicker than markers, her feet no bigger than the tip of a finger. Annabelle slid her finger into the tiny grip of her hand, pressed her palm to the bottom of her baby's foot.

Her baby. Her Olivia Caroline. Olivia MacDonald. Annabelle had promised herself that Olivia MacDonald could be whatever she wanted. That she would be strong and confident, unafraid to face her own fears. She would tramp through them like so much hay, kicking them aside as she went. She would never be the sort of woman who let a man hurt her.

Had she lived, Olivia would have been all those things and more.

Annabelle could still sometimes feel the weight of the pregnancy, the tingling of the breast milk as it rushed through her ducts. How she'd fought to hold onto Olivia, only relinquishing her to the nurses after they assured Annabelle that she'd see her baby again, ensure that she'd have a proper burial.

Despite the morgue's chill, Annabelle was suddenly hot. She forced herself to return the dead fetus to the drawer beside his mother. She checked that he wouldn't fall, then shed her gloves and let her coat slip off her shoulders. She peeled off her sweater, hung it on her chair, and pulled her coat on again, then took a long minute to wash her hands. She splashed water on her neck and blotted it dry with a paper towel.

Then, with a final look at the tiny form, she pulled the cotton sheet over the fetus and his mother and slid the drawer into the wall, leaving them to the cold and the dark.

On her way home, Annabelle left a long message for Hal. She

guessed Roger hadn't gotten to the glass yet, so she mentioned the notation in the doctor's file that said Reilly was supposed to be keeping tabs on her depression with her therapist. She also told him that she'd spent some time on Fischer and hadn't come up with anything new. "I've got the file with me to review at home tonight," she added, glancing at the computer on the passenger seat beside her. "I'll call you if I find anything interesting."

Annabelle stepped off the elevator in her apartment building with more than a little trepidation. She'd chosen this building for its high security, paid exorbitantly for the guarantee that every visitor was screened before being allowed beyond the lobby. But the memories of her pregnancy, of what Spencer was capable of, made her certain she was a fool to pretend he couldn't get to her here.

He'd gotten to her everywhere else.

Inside her apartment, Annabelle opened the cabinet for a bottle of wine and found it empty. She turned to the refrigerator, then remembered she'd never made it to the store yesterday. She'd been on her way to buy groceries after work when she was called to the scene. No wine, and she didn't have anything to eat for dinner. She opened the freezer and pulled out a package of chicken, frozen solid.

Spencer's housekeeper, Trudy, had made sure the kitchen was stocked. The house always smelled of fresh bread and lemons. God, what she wouldn't do right then for Trudy's Brunswick stew or a bowl of her she-crab soup. As she had many times in the past seven years, she wondered where Trudy was now, then pushed the thought away.

To appease her growling stomach, she pulled out rice cakes and peanut butter. Beside the grocery list was a sticky note reminding her to call PG&E about her electric bill, which had been astronomical this month. It was after six now, too late to call, and the bill was due tomorrow. Which meant rent was also due.

Exhausted, Annabelle retrieved the bottle of Evan Williams bourbon from the cabinet in the dining room and poured herself two fingers. It was one of the few remaining of her father's bottles and she was trying to make them last, but tonight she deserved a little splurge. Setting the bourbon on the table beside her dinner of rice cakes and peanut butter, she booted her personal computer and spent a few minutes catching up on her non-work emails and bills. With rent and utilities paid and her car insurance due to auto-deduct in three days, Annabelle calculated that she had $157 left in her account until the next payday, which was a week away. She swallowed the last of the bourbon and carried her dishes into the kitchen. As she debated another splash of bourbon, her cell phone rang. The number was unfamiliar, but a local area code. She took a full breath before answering. "Schwartzman."

"Dr. Schwartzman?"

"Speaking."

"This is Samantha Allen-Harker. I received your message today about Diane Reilly."

"Thank you for returning my call," Annabelle said. "I also faxed over a subpoena for Reilly's records."

"Yes," the therapist said. "I received that, too. Thank you. I apologize for not calling sooner. Most days I'm booked from eight straight through until six, so I'm just getting to my messages." She took an audible breath. "I have to admit, I was upset to hear the news."

Annabelle said nothing. She didn't deal with the death notifications—that was Hal's job—and she was self-conscious that she could say something wrong.

"She was such a bright young woman and she seemed on solid footing when I last saw her."

"So you were surprised to hear she'd committed suicide?" Annabelle asked.

Very," the therapist answered.

Annabelle pulled the top page—her grocery list—off the notepad and sat at the table. "When was the last time you saw her?"

"I was out of town last Thursday, so almost two weeks ago now. She was supposed to come in tomorrow."

Annabelle grabbed a pen, prepared to take notes. "And how did she seem at your last appointment?"

"A little down, I suppose, but that was to be expected with the break-up."

Annabelle's pen froze in mid-air. "Break-up?"

"Yes. When I saw her last, she said she and Peter were taking some time off."

Annabelle wrote "break-up" on her notepad and underlined it twice.

"You didn't know," Allen-Harker guessed.

"No."

"Well, perhaps something changed."

"Did she give you any idea why they were breaking up?" Annabelle asked.

"Pretty standard stuff. She was very consumed by the pregnancy—excited but also scared—how it would change her life, her career, finances, all understandable concerns. And Peter hadn't yet begun to really accept the reality of being a father. She wasn't sure he was ready to. As I said, this is all pretty typical, especially with a first child. The mother always experiences the sense of parenthood before the father because, of course, she's carrying the fetus around for nine months." She paused a moment and went on. "The odd thing is, I would have bet that they'd have gotten back together before the baby was born."

"Really? Why is that?"

"They'd been through a lot together. I think they really cared for each other."

"So you've met him?" Annabelle asked.

"Oh, yes. He came to some of her counseling sessions. He was very supportive; it was clear he was crazy about her." There was a momentary break in the connection. "I'm afraid I have to take this other call," Allen-Harker said.

"If it's all right, I may call with some additional questions," Annabelle said.

"Sure. Leave me a message if you don't reach me and I'll get in touch."

"Thank you so much," she said into the line, but the therapist was already gone.

She poured herself another finger of bourbon and stared down at the notepad where she'd written "break-up" and "crazy about her." She had outlined the word "crazy" while Allen-Harker spoke. But Annabelle suspected the woman hadn't really meant *crazy*—not the kind of crazy Annabelle was imagining.

For the next hour, Annabelle tried to work on her other cases, but couldn't focus. Giving up, she carried a pile of journals into the bedroom, dressed for bed, and settled under the covers to read an article about the use of electronic microscopy to measure enzymatic activity. The bourbon made it hard to keep her eyes open, and before long, she dropped the journal into the pile on the floor and shut off the light.

*

"Mrs. MacDonald," came Trudy's voice. Annabelle could picture the petite housekeeper as clearly as if she were standing in front of her. "You have to wake up."

Annabelle shook her head. She didn't want to wake up.

"Mrs. Mac," Trudy said again, her voice increasingly urgent.

At the old familiar nickname, Annabelle's eyes shot open and she bolted upright in the bed. It couldn't be Trudy. Trudy was in South Carolina. Trudy was from another life. Fumbling to switch on the bedside light, Annabelle knocked the empty glass off the table. It landed on the stack of medical journals before rolling across the hardwood. The light came on and she looked around frantically, her heart pounding. The room was empty. Her room, her San Francisco room. She rubbed her face. Trudy's voice had been so clear in her mind. Some kind of warning? That Spencer was close by, maybe? He'd found her in Seattle; surely he could find her here.

When Annabelle replayed it, she often found herself wondering about Trudy. Why had she come in that night? What had she seen or heard that made her risk coming into their bedroom and waking Annabelle up? She had never done that before.

Where was Trudy now? Annabelle couldn't believe she'd be working for Spencer. Not after what had happened that night. Her first memory was of waking to find Trudy, standing at the edge of the bed, shaking her gently.

"Wake up. Hurry!" Trudy whispered a third time, her voice pitched high in fear.

"What is it, Trudy? What's wrong?" Annabelle had asked.

But Trudy was already gone.

Unsure what was happening, Annabelle had remained in bed and feigned sleep. Holding her breath, she lay in the dark and listened for the slightest sound. The front door slammed shut, making the window-panes chatter in their frames. Spencer. She pulled the yellow covers to her chin and clamped her eyes shut. Maybe he would stop in the kitchen or his office, cool off before coming to bed.

Then he was in the bedroom. The door closed firmly and she could feel him standing motionless in the dark, testing her. He knew she was awake. He had a sick sense for those kinds of things.

"Come to bed," she said softly.

"I'm not tired." Though his words were sharp, she could hear the slur of alcohol.

She hesitated to respond. Perhaps it would have been better to try to pretend she'd been sleeping. Too late for that now.

The lamp in the corner of the room went on. "Come sit with me over here," he said. "I'll rub your feet."

Knowing she couldn't decline, she pushed the covers off and rose from bed, exhaustion making her nauseous. She moved toward him, trying to smile, but it trembled in the corners of her mouth.

Her husband had stepped out of his shoes and pulled off his tie, hanging it on the closet doorknob. She watched him unbutton his cuffs and roll up the sleeves, exposing those strong forearms. The motion filled her with dread. Their worst fights happened with his shirtsleeves rolled up. As if he were on the street, preparing for a fistfight. But when he looked up, his eyes were unreadable.

She moved to the small sitting area in the corner of the bedroom and sat down on the sofa, propped a pillow behind her, and stretched out her legs. He stopped undressing and moved toward her. She gave him a smile, tried to appear relaxed. He can smell your fear.

He didn't speak as he lifted her right foot onto his lap and began to rub his thumbs into the ball of her foot. Her arches ached from spending the day standing, first at the country club then later at the Bill Bryson reading.

Although her belly was large for sixteen weeks, it was her feet that bore the brunt of her pregnancy. They were distended and ugly, the blue veins below her ankles engorged like earthworms on wet pavement. Already she had been forced to buy shoes a full size larger than normal, and she wasn't yet halfway through her pregnancy. Spencer's thumbs moved in circles along the arch of her foot. The pressure was just right, and slowly the tendons started to loosen.

"That feels nice," she said, closing her eyes and letting her head fall against the cushion.

As though her comfort had goaded him, Spencer's thumbs began to move deeper, pushing now to the brink of pain. She tried to breathe through it, hoping he would ease up again, that it was just one of his tests. She didn't want a fight. But he struck deep into the tendon, sending an excruciating shock through her calf. She yanked her foot away. "Ow."

A smile danced on the edge of Spencer's lips.

"Let's go to bed," she suggested. "It's late."

She stood then and, when he didn't stop her, crossed to her side of the bed. Her foot tingled painfully when she put pressure on it, but she forced herself to walk as though nothing was wrong.

She sat on the side of the bed, pretending to work at a hangnail while she waited to hear him drop his clothes on the chair and disappear into the bathroom.

The room was eerily silent.

When she looked over her shoulder, she saw Spencer standing beside the bed, staring at the sheets.

Then she remembered.

She felt the gasp in her throat. It was Thursday and they hadn't changed the sheets. That must have been why Trudy had come into the bedroom. She'd remembered, too late.

Annabelle stood quickly. "Trudy must've forgotten."

Spencer stared at her across the bed, daring her to speak or move. She remained frozen, focusing on releasing the tension, as if she could, by sheer power of will, defuse the intricate bomb that was Spencer.

She didn't breathe, barely moved. She blinked, shifted her weight off her tender foot.

Spencer grabbed fistfuls of covers and tore them from the bed, throwing them to the floor with a snarl.

Still, she remained motionless. The extra sheets were in the hall closet. She would have to pass him. Go, she told herself, but she couldn't make herself move.

Spencer stood with his arms held away from his sides. His chest rose and fell with heaving breaths, and the tendons in his forearms danced under the skin as he moved his fingers.

"I can go get clean sheets," she whispered.

His gaze found hers, and she expected him to come at her, but instead he flicked one hand toward the door.

She moved briskly into the hallway. Her thoughts flickered to Trudy. Even from the maid's room at the rear of the house, she would be able to hear everything if she was listening. And Annabelle was certain she was listening tonight.

Her fingers slipped on the closet doorknob, the sounds of Spencer moving in the bedroom making her jumpy. She glanced at the stairwell. What would happen if she left? If she just walked out? She could go to her mother's.

No, not her mother. Ava. She could go to Ava, and—

"Bella."

She flinched at the closeness of his voice and yanked open the closet door, pulled a set of ironed sheets from the shelf. Yellow. The sheets were all yellow. She used to love the color yellow. How she hated it now. His hands gripped her shoulders as she pulled the sheets to her chest and turned back toward the bedroom.

He let her pass, but followed closely, silently. She set down the fresh linens and lifted only the fitted sheet, billowing it into the air over the bed and letting it fall. As it did, Spencer's face appeared again. Cold, hard. She looked away and tucked the top corner tight under the mattress, then the bottom one before circling to his side.

He caught her there, gripped her wrists, and pushed her until she stumbled backward.

"Spencer, it's late," she said, struggling to pull free.

His grip tightened until his hold burned her wrists. "You're awfully tired these days."

"I am," she said.

"Maybe you wouldn't be so tired if you hadn't gone to that reading tonight."

Annabelle closed her eyes. Of course he would bring up the Bill Bryson reading.

"Are you too tired for your husband?"

"No," she said. "Of course not."

His grip loosened.

"I'll make the bed and we'll visit," she told him. "I can tell you about the book reading if you want."

He let go of her wrists and rubbed his face, and she felt a flash of hope that the anger might pass. "You used to have more energy," he said.

"It's the pregnancy," she said.

He put his hands on her belly. "And we'll both be exhausted once she's born."

Annabelle frowned. What was he saying? "She'll sleep through the night before too long."

He said nothing, but kept his hands on the small, firm globe of her belly.

"I can sleep in the nursery for a while, too, so her feedings don't disturb you," she added.

Spencer's hands shifted to her waist and clamped down as his eyes met hers. "No."

"Okay," she said quickly. "It was just an idea."

"You'll sleep here?"

"Of course. I'd much rather sleep here," she said. "We'll work it out." She reached up to touch his face. "I can take care of both of you."

It took only seconds for the anger to wrench his jaw muscle and stretch the tendons in his neck.

"She's our girl, Spencer," she said slowly, trying to calm him down, to disperse the storm she could feel growing. "We'll love her together."

His entire body seemed to tremble as he shoved her backward. She caught herself on the bed, but he was on her again, yanking her up by one arm and spinning her around. She saw the two of them in the mirror above the bureau, him towering behind her. His face was scarlet, his mouth set in a terrible snarl. He stepped away, and for a moment, she believed he was going to leave.

But he came at her full force then, driving her forward. She tripped and he caught her, but rather than holding on to her, he gave her a final, violent shove. She struck the marble edge of the bureau belly-first. A wave of pressure exploded against her spine. She cried out, arching her back to fight the pain. Certain she would be sick, she dropped to the carpet. Gagged.

Spencer dropped to his knees. "Oh, Bella. Sweet Bella."

She held her belly with one hand, the pain coming in horrible crushing waves, and tried to stand up. Spencer placed his hands on her shoulders, but she shoved him away. "Don't touch me," she cried, pushing herself onto her hands and knees. The pain in her spine was tremendous and she had to fight to fill her lungs as tears streamed down her face.

Spencer sat back. "Bella, it was an accident."

She let out a sharp, harsh laugh but said nothing as she gathered her nightgown to stand. The fabric was wet against her hands, and she thought for a moment that the impact had made her pee. But then she realized.

"My water broke."

Outside her apartment window, an ambulance screeched in the night and Annabelle, again, scanned the room before kicking the covers off her legs and setting her feet on the floor. The clock read four-fifty. In the brisk morning air, she felt her chest and stomach. The flat of her belly, the rise of her hip bones on either end of the lifeless plateau, felt devastating.

There was no baby.

And there would be no going back to sleep now.

Two hours later, Annabelle poured herself a third cup of coffee and studied the tox and tissue reports on Reilly. Every ten minutes, she told herself she'd only spend ten more on the case before getting ready to go into the office. Everything confirmed the overdose and pointed to suicide. No other drugs or alcohol present in her system. She texted Hal to tell him what the therapist had said about the break-up. His response was immediate and definitive: *Nelson said they'd gotten back together.*

She was sure the boyfriend was lying, but Hal's next text said he'd confirmed the boyfriend's story with another of Reilly's friends. *Sounds like they broke up/got back together a few times.* She watched the bubbles at the bottom of the screen until another message popped up. *Any physical evidence that it wasn't suicide?*

She stared at the question for several moments before responding. *Not yet. Roger checked that glass?*

Yes. Negative for oxycodone residue.

Annabelle read the sentence twice. There was no drug residue in the bottom of the milkshake glass. Only in the victim's teeth. Her phone buzzed again, another text from Hal.

So she chewed 'em, right? On to Fischer…?

There was nothing else to do on Reilly. She had chewed the pills. No injuries to suggest anything had been forced on her. She had committed suicide. Case closed.

Annabelle forced herself to open her files on the Fischer case. She reviewed the report once more, confirming what she'd already found—the autopsy showed no physical evidence to link his death to a specific killer other than the mushrooms. No hairs or fibers were found on the body that could be matched to a worker from the kitchen. Nothing in the autopsy stood out as a way to narrow the pool of suspects. Furthermore, Fischer had high popularity ratings and was considered well-respected, so the police had been unable to determine a strong motive for the murder. Hal's team had cross-referenced other diners with the idea that maybe Fischer hadn't been the intended victim, but no one else seemed a likely target.

Annabelle considered the mushrooms. Someone had collected those specifically to use in killing Fischer. She texted Hal. *Collect shoes to check for soil deposits consistent with damp, forested areas?*

On it, came the reply.

As she went over the notes, the silence was broken by a toddler crying in the hallway. Annabelle's thoughts returned to the jagged crying of Diane Reilly's boyfriend, Peter Nelson. That crying… She set her coffee cup down. It reminded her of the way Spencer had cried, the only time she'd ever seen him really cry. Those choked sobs, the hoarse voice. Nelson had sounded the same way when she'd overheard him talking with Hal—calm, with a slight edge to his voice. "I answered that question, Detective," she'd heard him say. Exactly how Spencer had sounded that morning, speaking to the doctor in the hallway. Impatient, but normal.

Spencer's voice. "She lost a pregnancy, Gil. That's not like losing a baby."

Annabelle had stood frozen in the hospital room doorway, out of sight of the two men.

"Oh, I'm with you," the doctor said.

Had Spencer called him Gil? Did they know each other?

"But women react to these things differently than we do, Spencer."

"Well, you said it's too late, right? Please tell me the thing's been—"

Annabelle had been moving slowly forward, and she saw Spencer wave his hand in the air dismissively.

The doctor nodded. "The remains were cremated."

At the words, Annabelle gasped, her knees buckling beneath her.

Both men turned.

She'd reached for the door, stumbling back. Her lungs would not draw air and her vision went black as she fell. There were hands and voices and a prick in her arm. Behind it all, a violent ache carved into her chest.

She heard Spencer's voice. "What are you giving her?"

"Just a sedative," the doctor said. "It will help her relax, and a few hours of sleep will do a lot of good."

Annabelle struggled to open her eyes, tried to push them off her. "No!" She didn't want to sleep. She wanted to hold Olivia, to bury her. She wanted to bury her baby.

"I want to take her home. Let her rest in her own bed."

"I'm not sure that's a good idea, Spencer."

Even through the drug-induced haze, she knew the sound of Spencer preparing an argument. The words came more slowly, his voice lower, tinged with the stirrings of a growl. She tried to shake her head, to open her mouth to scream.

Tears flooded her eyes, but when she worked to lift her hand, it fell limply to her side.

"She'll feel better at home." She heard Spencer crying, shaky sobs. "Where I can take care of her, you know?" His voice was broken, raspy.

"Sure. I understand," the doctor said. After a brief pause, he lowered his voice. "It's against protocol, but I'll see if we can get her prepped to leave."

Spencer sniffed loudly. "Thanks, Gil. I'll make it up to you."

"You just take care of her and get back to work."

"Let's meet up next week," Spencer said, the hoarseness leaching out of his voice.

"I've got some ideas for your portfolio. Some emerging market stuff that we should take a look at. Real money to be made. Big money."

"Next week works."

"Call Karen and make an appointment, would you?"

"I'll do it. The charge nurse will be here in a few to get you signed out."

"Thanks, Gil." Then there was the sound of Spencer slapping the doctor's back, followed by the whisper of the door as it opened and closed.

Then the dark, pulling her in. She fought to rise to the surface. To shake it off. To stand, to scream.

"Don't worry, Bella," Spencer said, his lips pressed to her ear. "I'm going to take care of you. I'm right here." Warm, moist lips on her forehead, the sensation of his tongue flitting against her skin. "It's going to be you and me, Bella. Just you and me."

Was it possible that Peter Nelson was another Spencer? What had Diane Reilly been thinking when she went to sleep for the last time? Was she as horror-filled as Annabelle had been in the hospital in that moment, or had she found some sort of peace in her decision to take her own life and that of her unborn son? Annabelle had never once considered suicide. Running away, yes; stabbing her husband, yes. But never suicide.

*

The day went by slowly with only one autopsy to perform, an elderly woman found in her home. All unattended deaths required an autopsy, but this one was anything but suspicious. Eighty-nine years old, the woman had been a heavy smoker for more than sixty years; she had quit when her first great-grandbaby was born right after her eighty-first birthday. Aside from emphysema, she also suffered from congenital heart disease and liver failure. In the end, restricted blood flow to the heart caused by a thrombus had led to necrosis of the heart tissue and killed her. The paperwork for the case was quick, leaving Annabelle with the rest of the day free to focus on Fischer.

But she couldn't get her mind off Reilly. She called the lab to check on the rest of the evidence from the scene. If the boyfriend had drugged her, his prints might be on the prescription bottle or the milkshake glass, or maybe the blender.

"Lab."

Annabelle recognized the voice. "Naomi?"

"Yep."

"It's Annabelle Schwartzman. I hear you guys are a little crazy up there."

"Hi," she said with a sharp laugh. "Not just a little crazy. You should see this place. You looking for Roger?"

"Actually, maybe you can help. I was wondering if any of the evidence from the Reilly case was processed today?"

"Hang on and I'll check."

Before Annabelle could say anything else, she was listening to Pat Benatar singing "Love is a Battlefield." She wondered if Roger had chosen the eighties station for their hold music. She could picture that.

"Dr. Schwartzman?" Naomi returned to the line a moment after Annabelle had resigned herself to the fact that she would be singing Pat Benatar for the rest of the day.

"Yeah. I'm here," she said.

"We tested a glass from the bedside table for oxycodone. Contents were mostly water with some mint ice cream and chocolate residue but no presence of oxycodone."

"Right," she confirmed. "I heard about the glass."

"That's all we've done," Naomi said. "We've still got some other evidence to process—mostly fingerprinting, I think—but Roger marked the tox report on the contents of the glass as priority."

Annabelle wanted to ask if there would be time to run the other items for prints today, but something in Naomi's voice told her not to. Fischer was the priority across the department, and her uncomfortable hunch about an obvious suicide was hardly good cause to deflect resources from the directive. Instead, she thanked the young lab tech and replaced her desk phone in its cradle.

She stared at the Fischer file, then at the clock. It was one-thirty. *Okay,* she bargained with herself, *ninety minutes to work Reilly.* At three o'clock, she vowed, she would shift her focus to Fischer.

What could she do in ninety minutes? The lab was out. Hal was out. It had to be something she could investigate without help. Hal had mentioned he'd interviewed one of Reilly's friends. She could watch the interview, see if anything jumped out at her. That certainly seemed harmless enough.

When Annabelle found the video link in Reilly's case folder

and double-clicked on it, an error message appeared: "You are not authorized to view this content."

She didn't want to ask Hal to see it. He'd made it perfectly clear that he thought this case should be closed. She could stall it for another day in hopes that the lab would get to some of the other evidence, but she knew Hal was stressed about Fischer. Everyone was stressed about Fischer. Plus, what did the lab have that could help prove Reilly's death had been a homicide? If the boyfriend had killed her, would he have been careless enough to leave his prints on the prescription bottle? And if he had, the pills had been *his* prescription. Finding his prints on that bottle would not be conclusive evidence of foul play.

Cause of death was determined; that was where Annabelle's job ended. She had done her job. She should work on Fischer, but even if she *did* have any ideas to help the Fischer investigation, she couldn't deny her desperation to watch Hal's interview of Reilly's friend. The truth was that she couldn't let it go. Because it still felt wrong. *Because the boyfriend had reacted like a man who's been hunting me for seven years.*

No. She was not going to say that to Hal. She had to find a way around him.

Glancing at the phone, Annabelle had another idea. She dialed the main extension for the department and asked to be connected to sex crimes.

"Is Jamie Vail available?" she asked when the department receptionist answered. "This is Dr. Schwartzman from the morgue." Annabelle had gotten to know Jamie Vail on another case. Under the same circumstances, she was confident that the sex crimes inspector would have done exactly what she was doing. Or that's what she told herself now.

There was a pause and a series of beeps. She waited patiently, grateful for the absence of eighties music. No more than a minute later, she heard another click. "Schwartzman," came Jamie's voice. "What are you working on?"

"I've got a favor, actually."

"Tell me."

Annabelle explained about the video she wanted to watch but couldn't access.

"And I assume you're calling me because you don't want to ask Inspector Harris."

"That is true."

Jamie laughed. "Because he would have your head for not working on the Fischer case."

Annabelle exhaled. "Yes. I did the autopsy on Fischer, and I've been through my notes on it over and over. I just can't—"

"Don't sweat it," Jamie interrupted. "We're all sick to death of that guy. One less politician, where's the loss?"

Annabelle laughed. "So you don't mind helping?"

"Of course not," Jamie said. "I can access the video from here. You in the building?"

"In my office. I can be there in ten minutes."

"Great," Jamie said. "See you then."

Annabelle barely got the phone on the hook before snatching her jacket off the back of her chair and rushing out of her office.

She found Jamie standing in the tiny closet the sex crimes department used as a combination copy room, kitchen, and supply area. She was pouring coffee into a mug that read, "My other car is a broom." When she saw Annabelle, she smiled. "That's record time from the morgue."

"I really appreciate it," Annabelle told her.

"Bad coffee?" Jamie offered.

She shook her head. "Already had mine for the day."

Jamie returned the pot to the warming plate, then led Annabelle past the department desks and down a short hallway. "No one's using the viewing room, so we can set you up there." Jamie put her coffee down and signed into the computer. When the video was cued up, she stepped aside. "It's all yours. Ready to play."

Still wearing her coat, Annabelle thanked Jamie again and slid into the chair. She felt both excited and guilty. This wasn't her case anymore. Hal had told her to walk away. She glanced at her watch. It was ten to two. She still had seventy minutes to spend on Reilly. Seventy minutes to unearth *something* to prove to Hal—and to herself—that the wild goose chase was more than just baggage from her own past.

She pressed play and watched Hal appear in the center of the screen, leaning across the camera to adjust something. When he stepped away, an attractive Asian woman was visible at the table. Sitting with her hands folded on the table as Hal settled in across from her, she appeared to be close to the same age as Reilly, in her late twenties. While he situated his notebook, she stole glances at him, and Annabelle couldn't tell if she was simply nervous or if she found him attractive.

The first few minutes of the interview covered basic questions—name, address, how long she'd known the victim. Friends since grammar school, Tina Chang and Diane Reilly had remained close through high school and roomed together for their first semester at University of the Pacific. Tina reported Diane had met Peter Nelson when she and Diane were sophomores; he'd been a junior. Diane and Peter dated off and on for the spring semester of her sophomore year, most of her junior year, and had grown serious when she was a senior.

"Can you describe their relationship?" Hal asked.

Tina paused a moment. "He was kind of intense, but they were good together."

Annabelle leaned forward in her chair. The word "intense" would always make her think of Spencer.

"Intense?" Hal asked.

"In a good way," Tina said. "He wasn't an average college fraternity boy. He was really smart and did well in school…he took all sorts of crazy math and engineering classes. But even with his workload, he was always doing things for her—planting romantic notes and little gifts in the apartment, or planning dates for outdoor concerts or to go camping up in Portland or Seattle. She used to joke that he was her Prince Charming."

"And what did you think?" Hal asked.

"They seemed like a good fit. She was more chill, and I think she helped him relax and enjoy things."

Hal glanced down at his notes. "You mentioned on the phone that they'd broken up and gotten back together several times."

Tina nodded. "Like I said, he was serious and that was hard sometimes. But they always ended up back together."

"And did she ever express any fear of him or say anything to indicate he had ever hurt or threatened her?"

As Hal was asking his question, Tina was already shaking her head. "No," she said when he finished talking. "Never. Nothing like that."

A minute passed while Hal skimmed his notes. Then he asked if there was anything else Tina wanted to add, but again she shook her head. Hal rose from his chair and stepped in front of the camera and a moment later, the screen went black, the video over.

Annabelle blew out her breath.

"Prince Charming." The man she thought might have killed his pregnant girlfriend was described as a Prince Charming. The video reset to the start and she considered watching it a second time, but what would she gain? Tina hadn't hesitated on any of the questions; she didn't catch herself and change her answers. Tina said Peter Nelson was a good guy. Intense, perhaps, but for Diane Reilly, he had been Prince Charming.

She wondered if Tamara Whitman, the woman at the country club, the one Spencer had so wanted her to emulate, would have described Spencer the same way. He might have seemed intense but romantic, too. He had wooed her before their wedding, showed up with gifts and planned romantic dates. There had been moments in their relationship when he had seemed like a real-life prince. Even to her.

One day in particular, she'd been certain he was something from a fairytale. It was still early in their courtship, and Spencer had picked her up in a limousine. For three hours, they'd traveled behind blacked-out glass, talking and laughing while Spencer poured them tiny glasses of champagne and refused any clue as to where they were going.

"It's a surprise," he kept saying, but the blackened windows had made her feel slightly nauseous—as if they were in the hull of a boat without windows.

When they finally stopped, Spencer blindfolded her and led her out of the car.

"I'm afraid I'm going to trip and fall on my face," Annabelle said, her arms stretched out in front of her. Her heart raced erratically. "Do I really need the blindfold?"

"Yes," Spencer told her, chuckling. That had been back when his laugh gave her butterflies.

"I didn't have to wear it in the car."

"That's because you couldn't see where we were going, Bella," he said.

"I really don't like surprises."

"I know. That's precisely why you're getting one," he said in his coy voice. "We're almost there now. Five, maybe six more steps."

She had walked forward awkwardly. Despite the unnerving sensation of being blindfolded, she was unmistakably giddy at the adventure. Not to mention relieved to be out of the house where her mother was always asking questions about their relationship, always pushing and prying. She and Spencer had argued three days before—the biggest argument they'd ever had—and it had left her feeling unharnessed and slightly afraid. Her mother's constant badgering made it worse.

It had seemed like a minor thing when the conversation started. She'd left Duke the previous fall after her father passed away unexpectedly, and she wanted to finish her college education. Getting her degree wasn't the problem; Spencer always seemed charmed by her intelligence. They passed many evenings discussing foreign policy, usually in regard to how it might impact the foreign stock markets and his clients' investments. All she wanted was to finish school at Duke. But Spencer insisted that Greenville was as good a school—and they could be together. The idea that she wanted to be at Duke incensed him, as though the choice was not between two schools but between Spencer and some other man.

"Ready for the surprise?" he asked, still holding her hand.

"Yes!"

He let go of her hand and a moment later, the blindfold lifted. They stood in the driveway of a huge stone mansion. She scanned the street, but she had no idea where they were. "Whose house is this?"

"The main house belongs to clients of mine."

"What—"

"Patience, Bella," he said, pressing a finger to her lips. With that, he led her down the driveway to a black wrought-iron gate. There, they crossed a narrow path and arrived in a small, private side yard with a stone patio and four Adirondack chairs circling a table. Behind the patio was a carriage house. Vines climbed across its stone façade and bright blue shutters adorned the windows.

Spencer walked straight to the front door and turned the knob, pushing it open. Then he stepped back and waved her forward.

"Spencer, what on earth is this all about?"

"Go on, Bella."

Her heart raced, some combination of excitement and also an undeniable fear. Was he asking her to live here with him? Would she react wrong and ruin it? And where were they? Unless they'd been driving in circles, they'd come too far to be in Greenville.

She walked into a sitting area, beautifully decorated.

Spencer pointed to the table. "Go look."

She crossed the wood floor and found an envelope with her name on it. Pulling it open, she drew out a single sheet of paper. Confirmation of her registration for the fall semester. At Duke.

She spun around. "What?"

He was grinning. "You want to finish at Duke? Then that's exactly what you'll do."

"Spencer!" She wrapped her arms around him and kissed his neck as he laughed.

When she let go, she looked around. "Wait. Are we in Durham?"

"Clever girl," he said with a wink.

She scanned the room again. "Is this where we're staying tonight?"

"Yes. But not just tonight," he said, wrapping his arms around her waist. "I've arranged with Tim and Sonia that you can live here while you attend school this year."

"Really? Oh my God, it's so gorgeous."

"I'll fly up on the weekends to stay, and you can come home some weekends, too. It's nine months."

"A month for Christmas break, so really only eight."

He smiled. "Even better."

"I can't believe I get to live here." She turned back to him. "But it's probably so expensive."

He shook his head. "You've got two things to focus on while you're here."

"School?"

He nodded.

"And you."

He smiled. "Planning our wedding, actually."

Annabelle heard herself make a screeching sound as she watched

Spencer drop to one knee. "Annabelle Caroline Schwartzman, will you marry me?"

What woman could possibly say no to that? She had gotten her degree from Duke and the perfect man.

"You get anything useful?"

Annabelle turned to see Jamie standing in the doorway of the viewing room, and her thoughts returned to the video. "The friend said he was like Prince Charming."

Jamie watched her, cocking her head a little to one side. "But you believe otherwise?"

"I don't have any evidence," she admitted.

"Better go get some," Jamie said.

Annabelle stood slowly. "Yeah. That's the problem."

"Keep turning the rocks over," Jamie said. "If there's something there, it's bound to crawl out sooner or later."

Annabelle wanted desperately to believe that was true. "If he did kill her, maybe he's not so squeaky clean. You want to check this guy's record for me?"

"Of course," Jamie said. "Running rap sheets on douchebags is one of my favorite hobbies."

The two women returned to Jamie's desk where Annabelle gave her Peter Nelson's name and the address of his residence with Diane Reilly. "That's all I've got," she admitted.

"Should be enough," Jamie said. She hit enter and found Peter Nelson in the database, then clicked on his name. "Okay, it'll take a few minutes."

But a minute later, a form showed up on the screen. Nelson's name and address were at the top; most of the rest of the page appeared blank.

"That was fast," Jamie said.

Annabelle skimmed the page. "It doesn't look like much."

"It's not," Jamie confirmed. "Guy's pretty clean." She paged down. "We've got one incident back in 2005. He was nineteen, but the charges were dropped."

"Can you tell what the charges were?"

"Let's see if we can pull up the police report." Jamie switched to another system and entered a long report number into a search field. She hit enter and the screen read, "No matching result found." She typed it in again. "No matching result found."

Jamie groaned.

"What is it?" Annabelle asked.

"It's too old."

"Too old?" she repeated. "You mean, the record doesn't exist anymore?"

"Oh, it exists," Jamie said. "It's on microfiche somewhere."

Annabelle exhaled. "Okay. Well, I appreciate the help anyway."

Jamie put a hand up. "Hang on. I've got someone who might be able to help us." She lifted her department phone and dialed a number from memory. A few seconds passed in silence while Jamie stared up at the ceiling. Then she sat forward. "Brenda? It's Jamie Vail." A brief pause as Jamie nodded, then laughed. "I know. I'm going to owe you another one here in a minute. You're going to have to start collecting on those drinks," she said, grinning at Annabelle. "You up for pulling an old report for me?" A beat passed. "2005." Jamie read the report number into the phone. "Awesome, Brenda," she said. Then, with a final laugh, Jamie hung up.

She launched her mail app, and she and Annabelle chatted while they waited. A few minutes later, an email appeared.

"Wow," Annabelle said. "That was fast."

"Brenda's a whiz with the old files." Jamie double-clicked on the email attachment and Annabelle leaned in to skim over her shoulder. The report was dated June 3rd, filed by an Andrea Stanley.

"Shit."

"What?" Annabelle asked, trying to find the charge.

Jamie pointed to a box on the report. "According to this, Nelson's girlfriend of three years said he roofied her."

"He roofied his girlfriend?" Annabelle repeated.

"Andrea Stanley, nineteen, said she woke at 4:30 p.m. Saturday, June 3rd with no memory of getting home from the bar the night before," Jamie read.

Annabelle followed along on the screen as Jamie continued. "When she asked her boyfriend, Nelson admitted that he had roofied her to—quote—see what she would be like when she was fucked up—end quote." Jamie shook her head. "Jesus Christ. Some Prince Charming."

Annabelle's mind was reeling. He had drugged a girlfriend before Diane Reilly. "Can you print that out for me?"

"Sure thing."

Annabelle folded the police report and held it to her chest. "Thanks so much for the help, Jamie."

"Any time. Hope you nail that asshole."

On the way back to the lab, Annabelle took a deep breath and dialed Hal's mobile number.

"You got something?" he asked in lieu of "hello."

"You need to look at Peter Nelson again," she said, breathless.

"Nelson? Who's—" Hal stopped. "What? No. Not Reilly," he said, sounding exasperated. "We're working Fischer."

"He roofied his girlfriend before Reilly."

"How do you know that?"

"There's an old police report," she admitted.

"You're saying Nelson was convicted of dosing a girlfriend with roofies?"

"No," she admitted. "The charges were dropped, but—"

"Schwartzman," Hal said flatly, and his use of her last name let her know he was more than a little frustrated.

"I've got a gut feeling on this, Hal."

"Based on what? Roger checked the glass and the blender. There was no drug residue. She chewed the pills. She overdosed. I don't know if she didn't want a baby or if she was depressed or what—"

Annabelle stopped in the hallway. The residue in the teeth was definitely evidence against the theory that she'd been killed. How could he have gotten her to chew those pills? The residue might also have ended up in her teeth if he had crushed the pills into her milkshake—but if he'd done that, there would have been traces of oxycodone in the glass. She remembered the watery appearance of the milkshake residue in the glass. Nelson had probably rinsed it out.

Then she realized where the evidence might be.

"Are you still there?" Hal asked.

"We need to check the straw."

"What?"

"He could have washed the glass thoroughly enough to rinse out the drug residue," she said, "but he might have forgotten the straw. I've got to convince Roger to check it—then I'll stop."

"Come on," Hal said, sighing. "Roger is working on Fischer. We're *all* supposed to be working on Fischer."

"Just one more thing," she said. "The straw."

The line was silent a beat.

"Please," she added.

"Fine," Hal said. "I'll meet you in the lab."

She ended the call, then jogged down the stairs, ran through the hallway, and punched through the lab door, making it slam against the inside wall. It was more crowded than she'd ever seen it and every face turned toward her. "Sorry," she said, raising a hand in apology. She scanned for Roger and spotted him standing beside the long table at the far end of the room. As she approached, she noticed the surface was lined with knives, each one bagged and laying on an evidence sheet. There must have been at least fifty of them.

"I'm so sorry to barge in," she said quickly, scanning the counter.

"I know we're all working Fischer, but I need you to check the straw in the Reilly evidence."

Roger set down the knife he was holding and picked up another. "I can't right now."

"Please," she said. Tears stung her eyes and she blinked hard to keep them from falling. The whole room was still staring at her. "Please," she said, dropping her voice, fighting to pull herself together. "It's really important."

Roger stared at her for a moment.

"I wouldn't ask if it wasn't."

A second passed, then he gave a small nod. "Naomi," he called across the lab. "Will you pull the plastic drinking straw from the evidence on Reilly? It should be in refrigeration. Just the straw, please."

Annabelle exhaled.

"Scott," Roger said, moving past her, "will you clear off some space over there? I need to run a quick test on another case."

They moved around her, and Annabelle stood frozen where she was for fear that any movement might make Roger change his mind.

A couple of minutes later, Naomi returned with a paper sack and handed it to Roger. He carried it to the space Scott had cleared. "Come on, Dr. Schwartzman," he called to her. "Let's see what's in the straw."

Heart pounding, she crossed the lab and stood at Roger's side in silence as he updated the evidence log and cut open the sealed paper sack. The straw slid out onto a piece of fresh butcher paper Scott had put down. Roger pulled on gloves, then used a pair of thin needle-nose scissors to cut down the center of the straw. She wanted to lean over and look but forced herself to remain still, feeling foolish. If she was wrong, neither Hal nor Roger would ever trust her instincts again. But she had to know.

That moment, the lab door flew open a second time as Hal strode into the room.

"He's checking the straw," she told him, unable to hold his gaze.

Unfazed by the interruption, Roger fixed clips to both ends of the straw, splaying the plastic.

From where she stood, she could see bits of dark residue. Chocolate. No white. God, she didn't want to be wrong.

Hal stood beside her, his arms crossed. She tried not to move; she barely let herself breathe.

Roger lifted the cutting board and set it under the magnifying glass.

Afraid to meet Hal's gaze, she focused on Roger. All around the room, she realized, everyone had stopped to watch them.

After a few moments, Roger stepped back. "You want to take a look?" he asked.

She cringed.

"Come on," Roger said.

She approached the magnifying lamp and peered down, seeing the bits of chocolate through the tears of shame in her eyes. God, she was an idiot. Just because Spencer was a monster… She blinked to focus—then she saw it. Little bits of white chalky residue, camouflaged by the white of the straw. She exhaled, then turned to Roger, threw her arms around him, and hugged him. "Thank you."

Hal stepped up to the lamp to see for himself. "I'll be damned," he whispered after a moment. To Roger, he asked, "Any chance that's just backwash from pills she chewed?"

"Not likely," Roger answered. "If that was the case, there would have been drug residue in the glass, too."

Hal glanced at Annabelle and rubbed his head before addressing Roger. "So what happened? Why didn't we find the drug in the glass?"

Roger shrugged. "Someone must have washed that glass out pretty thoroughly. Blender too, if that's how the pills were crushed, but I doubt it. It would be tougher to be sure he could get all the remnants of the oxy off the blades."

"But it was milky," Hal said. "Like it still had the remnants of milkshake in it." He glanced at her. "Right?"

She nodded.

"The blender still had some milkshake at the bottom, right?" Roger asked.

"Right," Hal agreed.

"So maybe he washed the glass, then poured more of the milkshake in it to make it appear as though it was the original glass?" she suggested.

"You'll have to get him to tell you," Roger said to Hal. "But whatever he did to the glass, he didn't think to rinse the straw." Roger returned to the straw and studied it for another long moment. "Or it's possible that the contents had dried out enough to adhere to the plastic even after the straw was rinsed."

Hal had pulled his phone from his pocket; he dialed and then pressed the phone to his ear. A moment later, he said, "I need to get a patrol car over to the address on record for Peter Nelson. It's on Filbert Street."

"1407," Annabelle supplied. The address was seared into her brain.

"1407 Filbert Street," Hal repeated. He ended the call and slid the phone into his pocket. "Guess I've got to go chat with Mr. Nelson."

"Thank you, Hal," she said.

"Don't thank me, Anna," he replied. She felt a little better—he'd used her name. Actually, *his* nickname for her. Everyone else called her Schwartzman or Annabelle. "You're the one who caught him," Hal went on, then he made a sound like a short laugh. Shaking his head, he walked out of the lab.

Annabelle watched until the door closed and turned to Roger. "He's stressed on the Fischer case. He was really hoping this one would be easy."

"Don't worry about him," Roger said. "It's a little bruise to the ego. He'll survive."

She thanked him again and walked shakily toward the lab exit.

"I guess now you *can* get back to the Fischer file," Roger called across the lab.

She laughed. "I'm on it."

There was no word from Hal for the rest of the afternoon. And after another hour on the Fischer file, she still had nothing new to add. She had already decided there would be no work tonight. Instead, she was going to stream a movie: *27 Dresses*, the movie Diane Reilly had been watching when she died.

She wondered if Reilly had threatened to leave her boyfriend. Was that what drove him to kill her? What would have happened if Spencer had told her he didn't want the baby—if, instead of causing a miscarriage, he had asked her to abort the pregnancy? Would he have killed her if she had refused?

When they were trying to get pregnant, Spencer had wanted the baby as much as she did. Or he had seemed to. Was that another lie, another way he had imagined he would hold onto her? She wished she knew if Reilly had stood up for her child. Had Nelson discussed the options with Reilly? Or had he, like Spencer, simply robbed her of the choice? She tried to imagine what would have happened if she hadn't left Spencer. Would there have been another pregnancy? Another miscarriage? Had she escaped Reilly's fate by leaving Spencer three days after the miscarriage?

Spencer had woken her that morning to say he had invited her mother to dinner. Sitting on the bed beside her, he brushed her hair from her face, kissed her forehead. She hadn't spoken to her mother, so she assumed Spencer had told her about the miscarriage.

"You should make your jambalaya," he suggested gently. "Trudy can help."

She nodded but said nothing.

"You'll feel better if you get up and move around," he said, as if he were nursing her back from the flu instead of from killing her child. "You got quite a few callers yesterday, too," he added. "Your friends are worried about you."

She opened her eyes to look at him, studied his face. How could he seem so innocent? His eyes were wide and glassy, too. Did he feel any grief?

He stroked his thumb between her brows to erase the furrow there. "I'll check on you at lunchtime."

"I'm going to meet Tamara Whitman," she announced, the lie slipping off her tongue like melting ice.

"You are?"

"Yes," she said, holding his gaze. "She wants to take me to brunch and maybe do a little shopping." She blinked, still watching him. "I probably should cancel, though."

His brow furrowed. "Cancel? Why?"

"I don't have anything for dinner. I need to go shopping if I'm going to cook."

"Don't be silly, Bella," he said, pressing his lips to her temple.

She squeezed her eyes closed, her stomach sick and tight.

"Trudy will take care of dinner." He studied her face. "I'm so glad you have plans."

She offered him a smile. "Me too."

He laughed lightly, kissed her. "You scared me, you know?"

"I scared you?"

"At the hospital." He brushed the hair off her face. "When you fainted..."

Tears burned in her eyes, thoughts of her baby. She would not cry. "I'm okay now."

He watched her for a moment and she nodded again, forcing a wider smile to reassure him.

"Okay, then," he announced, standing. "I'll check in later to let you know what time I'll be home."

"Perfect. Have a good day."

"And you enjoy your girl time. Buy yourself something pretty from me."

"I will."

She glanced at the clock. Spencer had left later than she'd hoped. It would be close to ten before she could get out the door. Still, she knew exactly what she would pack, so it didn't take long to pull her things together. She couldn't risk leaving the house with anything larger than a gym bag in case a neighbor saw her. She kept her wedding ring on, but left her other jewelry out on the bathroom counter, the way she often did. She took the bare minimum—nothing to indicate that she was planning to be gone for longer than an afternoon.

Even if Spencer started to wonder where she was, he wouldn't want to call Tamara or Gregory and admit he didn't know where his wife had gone. He would never want someone to guess there was something wrong in their perfect marriage. There was a risk that he might mention it to Gregory during the course of their day, but that felt unlikely. Either way, she'd be gone. Her car would be parked at the airport and she had seven hundred dollars in cash—every penny of emergency money she'd saved up—to convince a taxi driver to drive her to Ava in Charleston. She knew her aunt would welcome her; she would put herself in Ava's hands. Ava would help her. From the start, her father's sister had been distrustful of Spencer. If only Annabelle had seen what Ava had.

As she drove out of the neighborhood, she saw Spencer pass, in the opposite direction. His gaze held hers and fear rose from her gut and tightened around her throat. A moment later, her phone rang. She was terrified he would ask her to come meet him or tell her to come home. She couldn't turn back. Not now.

"Hi." She clenched the steering wheel, fear hot in her belly, heart racing. "I was surprised to see you. You heading to the house?" Her voice sounded breathy to her own ears.

A pause on the line. "I forgot a couple of files for a client meeting, so I had to come back," Spencer said. "You're leaving earlier than I expected. And why were you driving out toward Augusta? You said you were meeting Tamara in town."

"I am." She glanced at the clock. "We're meeting at eleven."

A long pause stretched across the line. Though he said nothing, his accusations sliced silently through the air.

"One of my tires looks a little flat," she said. "I'm just stopping at the gas station. I didn't know how long it would take and I didn't want to keep her waiting."

"It won't take an hour to check a tire," he said, like she was an idiot, then sighed. "I'll come take care of it for you."

"I'm fine," she said, regaining the strength in her voice. "You've got clients to meet."

"I'm coming now," he insisted. "You're going to the Chevron station?"

There was no telling him not to come. "Yes."

"I'll be there in three minutes. Wait for me."

Her pulse pounded so intensely she could feel it in her teeth and nose. She punched the gas pedal and swung through a yellow light onto Augusta, then sped the two blocks before crossing the double lines and barreling into the Chevron parking lot. She raced past the pumps and stopped abruptly beside the air station. With the engine shut off, she yanked the keys from the ignition and jumped out of the car, leaving the door open. As she moved, she scanned the street for his car. He would be two or three minutes behind. If he was telling the truth about where he was—but what were the chances that he was telling the truth?

Trembling, she knelt beside the front tire on the driver's side and twisted the black stem cover off the tire's air valve. She thought of her bag in the trunk. What if he went to open the trunk? How would she explain? At least she was dressed for a lunch—except her shoes. She was wearing tennis shoes. The black valve cap rolled out of her shaking hand and under the car.

She let it go, focused on pressing the point of her house key to release air from the tire. Held it down for one, two, three. One and two again. Then she dropped to her hands and knees and searched for the black cap, which had rolled under the hood. She had to lay almost flat on her belly to reach it. Hands trembling, she twisted it on, then stood and swiped her palms across her slacks.

She needed different shoes. Spencer would know she wasn't going to lunch in tennis shoes. He would never allow it. A cold damp sweat on her neck, she checked the road. There was no sign of his Lexus. How much time did she have left? Maybe thirty seconds? She ran to the trunk and used the fob to pop it open, then grabbed hold of her bag and yanked the zipper. Her pulse drumming in her throat, she dumped the contents of the bag into the trunk, shaking it until her sandals fell out. Her stomach cramped and she gripped it, trying to breathe through the pain. A quick glance at the road showed no sign of his car. Keep moving, she thought. Leaving her things strewn across the trunk, she slammed it closed and returned to the driver's seat, pulling the door closed behind her.

As she twisted around to check the road, Spencer's car drove through the intersection. She patted the sweat from the back of her neck, checked her face in the mirror. Gasped at the sight of a black streak beside her nose. Licked her thumb and rubbed it away.

She froze as Spencer parked beside her and stood slowly from the car, looking around before approaching.

She watched his face for signs that he knew what she was doing. How would he know? How did he ever know? She cracked the door and waited until he was beside the car. He scanned her outfit, stopping when his gaze reached her shoes.

"For driving," she said, lifting her sandals off the passenger seat to show him. "My feet are still a little swollen."

Spencer nodded, taking in the inside of the car, sweeping across the back seat. He put a hand on the top of the car, body pointed toward the trunk. What was going through his mind?

"I thought that front tire was low," she said, pointing.

Spencer's gaze was slow to shift to the tire. He stalked the length of the car and bent beside the tire. "Doesn't look low to me."

She felt a wave of fear. "Really?" she said, stepping out of the car. Keeping her distance, she glanced at the tire, which was clearly low on air. "I can drive on it?"

"Definitely," he said. "It's exactly like the others."

She glanced at the back tire, then at the front. Just go with it, she thought. Don't argue. She only had to make it to the airport. After that, she'd never see this car again. "Well, that's good," she said. His eyes were pinned on her. "I thought maybe I'd picked up a nail or something."

He didn't look at the tire. "No nail." He closed the distance between them, pressed his lips to her cheek. "You feel warm," he said. "You sure you're feeling okay?"

"Yeah. But I'll take it easy today."

"You should."

She turned to her car.

"I'm going into town. I'll follow you."

She nodded.

"Just to make sure that tire's okay," he added.

She reached out and touched his hand, her legs trembling. "Thanks for looking out for me."

Spencer's expression softened momentarily. "Of course," he said. Before he could say more, she sat in her car and pulled her seatbelt on. She waited until Spencer was in his car before starting her engine and reversing away from the air station.

As she drove toward town, she was careful of yellow lights, making certain she didn't accidentally lose him. When he made a left into his office parking lot, she waved out the window and drove to the town center.

She parked where she always did when she met friends for lunch. She put her sandals on, then got out of the car and walked the long way to the public library. She hid in the stacks for forty-five minutes before calling the main number at his office.

When the receptionist answered, she lowered her voice to a whisper and put on a gravelly Southern accent. "I was trying to reach Mr. Spencer MacDonald," she announced. "Is he in?"

"He is in the office, but I'm afraid he's on his line right now. Would you like his voicemail?"

"Yes, please," she answered, holding the line until she heard Spencer's voice on the recording. She ended the call and backtracked from the library to her parking place. There she silenced her cell phone and dropped it into a trashcan in the parking lot before making her way to the airport.

With every mile, she breathed more easily. The farther she got from Spencer, the more she told herself that the past no longer mattered, that she was moving forward. Away. Spencer might know people in Greenville, but his reach couldn't extend far. Probably not to Charleston, and certainly not beyond. Which was where she was going—way, way beyond.

*

How relieved she'd been when she'd arrived at Ava's house that day. How much better her life had been since she'd left Spencer.

She was two blocks from home when Hal called. "Hey," she answered, adjusting her earpiece.

"Well, you were right," Hal said, sounding breathless.

"He confessed?"

"He confessed," Hal repeated. "You got him with the straw, Anna. Soon as it was out there, he fell apart. He didn't want the baby, and she refused to terminate the pregnancy."

"He killed her because he didn't want the baby." Her mouth was suddenly dry and she lifted her water bottle from the cup holder to find it empty. She swallowed against something like sand in her throat.

"He claims he was trying to make her miscarry, not kill her."

She closed her eyes to the tears that burned at the thought of a man threatened enough by an unborn baby to kill both mother and child. She took a shaky breath.

That could have been her.

"Nice work," Hal said.

"You too," she said. "Thanks for letting me know."

"Sure," Hal said. A beat passed, and he asked, "You okay? You sound a little quiet."

"Just tired, I think."

"Sorry I was an ass about Reilly."

"You were," she said, teasing him.

"It's this Fischer thing. It's killing me."

"I know," she said. "Fischer's my priority now. First thing tomorrow."

Another beat of silence. "You sure you're okay?"

"Positive," she lied. "Just a big day."

"Okay. Get some rest."

"Will do," she promised. "I'll see you tomorrow."

She passed the remainder of the drive in silence, waving at the night watchman as she pulled into the secure garage.

One day she would tell Hal about Spencer, the truth of her marriage, how she'd lost her baby. She would share what it had been like to live with that monster—share it not only with Hal, but with others—close friends, a lover. She imagined the scene: They would be drinking wine and Annabelle would raise her glass and extend it across the table to clink with her guest's. "Thank God I'm done with him," she would say.

On that day, she would remember that she'd gotten justice for Diane Reilly. And maybe she'd even get justice for herself. Some day.

Please turn the page for a preview of book one of the
Dr. Annabelle Schwartzman Series, *Exhume*.

1

San Francisco, California

DR. ANNABELLE SCHWARTZMAN THREADED her half-circle number-five suture needle, the kind normally used in orthopedic surgery. Pinching together the edges of the Y-incision she'd made an hour earlier, she began the process of closing the victim's chest.

The chest and torso had been badly burned, and the fire left the skin fragile. Since there wasn't going to be an open casket, the standard protocol was to use staples to close the incision. Schwartzman preferred sutures. Staples were effective but seemed too industrial. The sutures were slower, and she enjoyed these last minutes with the victim, the time to fully process the death before contacting the investigator.

Both the intensity and the reward of the medical examiner's job were in being the final voice for a victim. Schwartzman was the last person to have access to the body, the one who decided if death was from natural causes or at the hand of another. It was intense and quiet work, the hours spent studying each piece in a puzzle that needed to be worked out.

In medical school, many of her peers chose specialties in order to interact with patients—gynecology for the joys of birth, or pediatrics for the children.

But those jobs came with sadness, too. Fetuses didn't always make it to full term. Children developed diseases and died.

As an ME, Schwartzman interacted with patients in the most intimate way—limitless in the depths she could go to diagnose a death. For many, forensic pathology would seem like an impossible choice. For her, it was the only one. People chose medicine for the heroics—to cure disease, save lives. In forensic pathology, there were no heroics. Just unanswered questions.

The overhead light shut off. She waved her arm in the air to trigger the motion sensor. After 7:00 p.m., the lights automatically turned off after ten minutes. The halogen in the corner crackled angrily as it flickered on and off before settling into a solid glow. The hallways were dark, the room silent.

Some of the department's other medical examiners worked with loud music, but Schwartzman appreciated the silence. One reason she enjoyed being in the morgue at odd hours.

She had been heading home from a dinner with some women from the police force when the morgue called to her, left her energized, ready for work.

She didn't go to the morgue because there was work—the work was always there. What she loved about the morgue was the space. The smell of the grapefruit lotion she used after she'd washed up and before she donned gloves, the vinegar scent of the clean instruments and table.

She always smelled these before the body.

The girls' night out with her coworkers on the force had given her a chance to talk to Homicide Inspector Hailey Wyatt, to get to know her away from the crime scenes they had worked together. Schwartzman had surprised herself by opening up about Spencer.

How long since she had done that?

Melanie in the last year of medical school—six and a half

years ago—that was the last time she'd allowed herself to get close to someone.

Her phone buzzed. A text from Hailey. **Glad u came tonight. See u tmrrw.**

Schwartzman smiled. She had felt a growing closeness. They might become friends.

Spencer kept her isolated, certainly while they were married but even after she'd escaped. He had planted the notion that he was always close—confiding in someone was offering a key that might be used against her.

Dinner hadn't felt that way at all. It was a relief to get her truth out there—a man she hadn't seen in more than seven years was stalking her. He'd made her believe her mother was in the hospital. Had managed to elude building security at her apartment and deliver a bouquet of yellow flowers. A color Spencer loved and she despised.

But he was a fool to think he could get to her.

She was with the police department. That bouquet of flowers was being processed by Roger Sampers—the head of the Crime Scene Unit himself. In only six months, San Francisco had started to feel like home. Here, for the first time, she had her own space. She was in charge of her own work, which gave her the opportunity to give it the focus it deserved and to excel at something she loved.

Because she was good; she was appreciated. She had the support of her peers. She had . . . friends. A ridiculous thought for a thirty-six-year-old woman, but there it was. She liked it here.

Seattle had always been temporary. The first city away from Spencer, a place to regroup, finish her training. Seattle was perfect for that period of her life.

She was a doctor now, ready to begin her career, put down roots. She had spent long enough looking over one shoulder. She was determined to stay in San Francisco, even more so after the evening with those women.

She made her final notes and signed off on the work. Her phone buzzed in her pocket as she was sliding the body back into the drawer. She snapped off her gloves and pulled the phone from her lab coat. *Hal.*

"You're psychic," she said in lieu of hello.

"Oh yeah?" Homicide Investigator Hal Harris said. In the six months they had worked together, she and Hal had created a comfortable banter that made cases with him her favorites.

"How's that?"

"I just finished our burn victim."

"And?" Hal asked.

"Autopsy showed massive bilateral pulmonary thromboembolism with pulmonary infarction."

Hal groaned. "English, Schwartzman."

"Natural causes," she said. "He died of massive blood clots in his lungs."

"Guy dies of natural causes, then drops a cigarette in bed and torches his own house." Hal had a knack for pointing out the ironies of their job, but they were always relieved when the autopsy revealed a death was due to natural causes.

"Yep. You want me to call Hailey?"

"No. I'll tell her," Hal said. "You ready for another one?"

"Sure," Schwartzman said. She was always game for another case. Lost in a case at the morgue, home alone with a book or occasionally an old black-and-white movie—usually one her father had loved—those were her best moments.

The distractions were all the more important now that Spencer had found her again. The phone calls, the creepy bouquet of yellow flowers that had appeared outside her apartment door. Worse was the fact that no one in the heavily secured building could explain how the deliveryman gained access to her floor. Seven years and five months since she'd left, and he would not give up.

"I'll text the address and send over a picture from Dispatch," Hal said. "I'm about five minutes out."

"I'll try to leave here in the next ten."

"Great," Hal said. "See you then."

She was ready to end the call when he said, "Hey, Schwartzman?"

"Yeah?"

"Nice work on that last one."

She smiled. Hal was good at praising his peers—herself, the crime scene techs, the patrol officers. It was another of his endearing qualities. "Thanks, Hal."

She ended the call and removed her lab coat, hanging it in her narrow locker. After exchanging the orange Crocs she wore in the lab for her street shoes, she packed up her case for the scene. Her phone buzzed with the address Hal had sent. She double-clicked on the attached image. Waited as it loaded.

The image came into focus.

A woman. About Schwartzman's age. Wavy, brunette hair. Laid out on her bed. Shivers rippled across Schwartzman's skin like aftershocks. Someone had already put a sheet over her legs and stomach, as though she'd been found nude, but a thin stripe of her clothing was visible above her waist. Other than the pale color of her skin, she might have been sleeping.

In her hands was a small bouquet of yellow flowers.

Read *Exhume* now.

ABOUT THE AUTHOR

Photo © 2018 Mallory Regan, 40 Watt Photography

Danielle Girard is the *USA Today* and Amazon #1 bestselling author of *Chasing Darkness*, the Rookie Club series, and the Dr. Schwartzman series—*Exhume*, *Excise*, *Expose*, and *Expire*, featuring San Francisco medical examiner Dr. Annabelle Schwartzman. Danielle's books have won the Barry Award and the RT Reviewers' Choice Award, and two of her titles have been optioned for movies. A graduate of Cornell University, Danielle received her MFA at Queens University in Charlotte, North Carolina. She, her husband, and their two children split their time between San Francisco and the Northern Rockies. Visit her at www.daniellegirard.com.